BLUE SAGE COU[NTRY]

When Bert Osborne was hired out to hunt cattle for old Amos Northfield, Snowy Baker told him there were no cattle and old Amos was crazy. Then came the fighting free-grazers, four manhunting outlaws and finally, Snowy and Bert discovered that old Amos was hiding a wounded outlaw on the ranch. That was the beginning of trouble which did not end until three men were dead—and something called 'the Spanish mine' cropped up to give more trouble but finally an incredible windfall.

BLUE SAGE COUNTRY

BLUE SAGE COUNTRY

by
BRUCE THOMAS

MAGNA PRINT BOOKS
Long Preston, N. Yorkshire,
England.

LARGE TYPE EDITION

British Library Cataloguing in Publication Data

Thomas, Bruce *1916—*
    Blue sage country.—Large print ed.
    Rn: Lauren Paine   I. Title
    813′.54(F)   PS3566.A34

    ISBN 0-86009-554-1

First Published in Great Britain by Robert Hale Ltd 1982

Copyright © 1982 by Robert Hale Ltd

Published in Large Print 1983 by arrangement with Robert Hale L⸍d London

Photoset in Great Britain by
Dermar Phototypesetting Co.   Long Preston, North Yorkshire.

Printed and bound in Great Britain by
Redwood Burn Limited, Trowbridge.

CHAPTER 1

THE BIG COUNTRY

According to Ute legend, the vast territory which was known as Blue Sage Range was once an enormous lake which reached all the way from the bald Rawhide Hills to the south, to the great, curving, forested horseshoe-shaped eastern, western and northern continuation of the Rocky Mountains in the other directions, and whereas Ute legends were colourful, appealing and spiritual, as Snowy Baker said before sundown as he and Bert Osborne made their ring of stones for the supper fire, a man didn't have to know a damned thing about

God or history or anything else, when each time he scooped a palmful of dirt it had shards of tiny seashells in it.

They had the horses hobbled, their camp carelessly established on a low rolling rib of land overlooking Blue Sage Range, and finished foraging for brush faggots to make a fire with just as the sun balanced atop a mighty peak of the black-veined distant rims.

They were closer to the northward sweep of huge mountains than they were to open country, but in an almost limitless sink like the blue sage country, any eminence at all provided horsemen with a view so immense and generally unchanging, and practically treeless, that if there was movement within twenty miles it would be noticeable.

Snowy Baker fired the twigs, which burned like all greasewood did, with a fiercely hot, smokeless flame, consuming themselves much more quickly than tree-wood did, and as he poked stones to have their coffeepot firmly balanced and scowled at the heat which singed his face, he said, 'That damned old man...He don't have any cattle out there. I doubt if he ever did have.' Then he backed away from the fire, frowning at it. He was a compact man with a short back, powerful sloping shoulders, oaken arms and slightly bowed legs. His hair was almost completely white, and his face was weathered into creases and lines, but he did not leave an impression of age, although he was probably in his forties.

He coughed when smokeless greasewood fumes reached him, turned away and looked over to where Bert was standing still, lean and motionless, gazing steadily out over the vast miles of blue sage and gritty ground.

'Hey! You still thinkin' about the Ute stories?'

Bert turned deepset grey eyes in a bronzed, strong face. 'Aside from the old man who runs stock out there?' he asked.

Snowy fished forth a blue bandanna to wipe his watering eyes as he replied and moved again, when that acidy, smokless scent reached him. 'There's some outfits run livestock out there, but mostly they're fifty, sixty miles southward, near them bald hills you saw before sunset.'

'No one ranges out, say a few miles, maybe five, ten miles?' Asked Bert, turning to gaze out there again.

Snowy sniffed, stowed his bandanna and glared at the intense little blue flame inside the fire-ring. 'I hate workin' in country where you got to use that damned wood to cook by...No; no one ranges out there. It belongs to Mister Northfield but he doesn't range out there, hasn't in twenty years, so they tell me.' Snowy produced the bandanna again, blew lustily into it, repocketed the cloth and then violently sneezed. 'Gawd-damn greasewood,' he exclaimed. 'What in the hell did I ever come back to New Messico for anyway?'

Bert Osborne must have heard the sounds of Snowy Baker's distress, but he acted as though he hadn't when he said, 'Well; someone is sure as hell runnin' cattle out there now,' and raised a long arm to point with. Snowy was perfectly willing to change course and get more distance between himself and the greasewood fire, so he walked over into the crumbly tan stone area where Osborne was pointing, and squinted. He sniffed again then said, 'I don't see anything. Antelope, Bert.'

Osborne lowered his arm slowly. He was a few inches taller than Baker and a number of pounds leaner. 'Can't see 'em now, light's failing, but they were out there, and it looked like a big bunch of 'em.'

'Antelope?'

'Cattle, Snowy.'

Baker made a sniffing sound and stalked the cooking-fire from a different direction. They made their meagre meal, had their coffee, rolled a couple of smokes and listened to the noisy yapping of nervous foxes south of them, which had probably picked up either horse-scent or man-scent.

It was a warm night, midsummer was well along throughout the blue sage country, there was a two-thirds old lop-sided moon looking indifferently unkempt amid all the meticulous order-liness of the high-curving heavens, and a few yards off where the hobbled horses picked grass, the only sound was of an occasional shod hoof grating over decomposed granite.

Bert Osborne was younger than Snowy Baker, but, again, it would have been impossible to pin down his age from looks; he, too, was a lifelong rangeman; they invariably looked older than they were. Fierce hot winds, driven sand, blazing suns, winter-burn, every aspect of raw nature turned youthful cheeks to bronzed leather after a few years. After perhaps as much as twenty or thirty years, a man's face *was* leather.

'Somewhere out there,' Snowy said quietly and thoughtfully, 'there's an old mine. The Spaniards when they come through here hundreds of years back riding mules for Chris'sake, made it, and after them come the Messicans... Then, when the greasers lost the Messican War with us and pulled out, the mine got lost.'

Bert eyed his companion by firelight. 'And it was full of gold, an' there was left behind a dead Spaniard in full armour to put a hell of a curse on folk who came by.'

Snowy grinned. 'Naw. If there was a curse they never told me about it.'

'Who told you there was such a mine?'

'Some Messicans I knew when I was a

kid workin' cattle on across in them bald hills.'

'Did they tell you where the mine was?'

'Naw. They didn't know. Just that it was out there, and the Spaniards found it first.'

'Did you ever go look for it?'

Snowy snorted. 'Hell, no. I got better things to do than go ridin' all over hell out there lookin' for somethin' that's likely all caved in and unrecognisable by now.'

Bert pitched his cigarette butt into the white-hot coals of their greasewood fire and ran a long glance up over the sky, then out where he could hear the horses contentedly searching for grass-stalks amid the crumbly shale and punky soil.

Snowy had something else to say. 'You don't know that old man. You're new to this country. Me, I've worked it off an' on for more years than I like to look back on.'

Bert stretched out alongside the stone-ring with his head propped on one arm. 'All I know is that when I came through, he hired me. He seemed sort of gruff, but fair enough. Made me a decent offer, agreed to pasture my private horse, and sent me down here to find some critters marked with a Mex hat on the left ribs.' Bert yawned and gazed at Snowy across the ring from him. 'He didn't tell me you were down here; didn't even tell me he had another man riding for him.'

Snowy lifted his hat to scratch, then reset the hat before speaking. 'Well, I only sort of ride for him. I've known the old cuss for maybe five, six years. It's his range down here and I was goin' to do a little mustanging this summer, so I asked permission to range over his country, and he agreed, an' even said he'd pay me if while I was horse-hunting I'd watch out for his cattle.' Snowy paused to lift his head a little and wag it.

'He hasn't had any cattle down here in the Lord knows how long.'

'You sure?' Osborne asked, returning Baker's sardonic gaze.

'Yeah I'm sure. I've ridden for just about every outfit in the blue sage country including the old man years back, and anyone'll tell you he only has maybe a hundred cows left, and they range north in the foothills above his home-place.'

Bert shifted position slightly as he pondered, then he said, 'He don't know his critters are up north in the hills?'

Snowy had no answer to that, but he said, 'Amos Northfield hasn't straddled a horse in years. What little goin' out he does, he does in an old wagon or an old top-buggy. I'd say he never knows exactly where his cattle are, unless he hires someone to find them for him.'

Bert plucked a curing grass-stalk and chewed on it for a while before speaking again. 'What you're saying is that

Mister Northfield is one brick shy of a load.'

Snowy spread his hands. 'Well hell, he's seventy-five years old.'

Bert chewed the stalk. 'My grandpaw was ten years old'n that and he could fork a horse, cuss a blue streak, and turn a bolter at full speed.'

Snowy had no answer to that, so he sighed, listened a moment to the horses, then said he was going to unroll his blankets. But before he turned in he looked around and said, 'You got two hunnert miles of blue sage to hunt in. Good luck.' Then he removed his boots, his gun and shellbelt, his hat, and went to bed. Just before going off to sleep he said, 'Antelope, that's what you say. Goodnight.'

Bert Osborne grinned and also went after his blanket-roll.

CHAPTER 2

THE MEETING

Dawn arrived early in the high desert country almost any time of year but particularly in early or mid-summer, and as Snowy Baker got the cooking-fire going again from more greasewood faggots Bert Osborne brought back from over where he had rehobbled the two saddle animals, the fresh, rather pleasant chill of early morning was beginning to diminish.

Bert said it was going to be a hot day, and Snowy, with both eyes closed against the greasewood fumes, made an observation based upon his past experience in blue sage country. 'An' it just keeps gettin' hotter from now on until you can fry an egg on a rock.'

Bert walked back to his crumbly vantage-point to peer southward. After a few minutes he returned, squatted to fill a dented tin cup with black coffee, and said, 'Cattle, not antelope. Go look for yourself.'

Snowy went, partly to get away from the greasewood fumes and partly to be able to tell Bert Osborne that he was as stubborn as a jackass.

He stood a long while out there. Once, Bert called, saying the meat was fried, then divided the food and sat with his back to the huge plain to eat.

Snowy eventually returned, hunkered down without a word, and reached for the tin plate with the nearly black, curly strips of refried meat in it.

Bert let enough time pass, and did not raise his head as he said, 'You satisfied now?'

Snowy chewed masterfully, swallowed with an effort and scowled across the fire. Well, last night it was antelope.'

Bert laughed. 'Sure; with red backs and wide horns. You're pigheaded. It was cattle last night and it's still cattle. Did Mister Northfield mention leasing his range to anyone?'

Snowy went back to eating. 'No, and knowin' him I'd say he didn't lease it. He's a strange old gaffer; he won't lease any land, even when he's not using it, but this country down here—he's real odd about it.'

'Then he's bein' grazed over,' stated Bert, finishing the meat and reaching for his dented cup again. 'Do we chouse them off or go back to the ranch and tell the old man?'

Snowy frowned. *'We?'*

'You said you worked for him,' stated Bert. 'Last night you told me—'

'What I said was—he give me the right to hunt wild horses on his range if

I'd keep an eye peeled for some Mex hat cattle.'

'That's workin' for him,' stated Bert Osborne. 'Besides, as long as there are cattle out yonder, and the men who'll be workin' them, you can forget finding wild horses.'

Snowy speared the last bit of shoe-leather meat with his clasp-knife, wolfed it down, put the tin plate aside and ranged a thoughtful, slightly indignant glance down over the miles of sage country. Then he swore with eloquence and feeling because Osborne was correct; if there had been mustangs out there, with the advent of cattle and man-scent there would not be a wild horse within fifty miles. Maybe three times that many miles. 'My summer's shot right square in the butt,' he exclaimed, drained his cup and arose to begin striking camp. 'All right. We'll go out there.'

They left the camp as it was, saddled

both horses and struck out down off the rolling landswell on to the sagebrush plain, and because as with all great distances, what they could see of browsing cattle, what appeared to be the near-distance turned out to be a lot more than that. The sun was high before they were near enough to make out individual cattle. It was still higher before they got down among scattered cattle and made their knowledgeable estimate.

'At least a thousand head,' surmised Bert, and Snowy agreed with that.

The animals had a road-brand, which meant that their original brand had not been vented; they had been marked with someone's temporary brand, so that, during a long cattle-drive, individual animals which might stray or become intermingled with other cattle on the open range, could be identified and reclaimed.

Snowy halted and sat his horse studying cattle on all sides. 'They're either free-grazers,' he opinioned, 'or drovers on their way to some particular territory'. He stood in his stirrups. 'If it's free-grazers, we better be careful.' He pointed. 'Yonder's a rider and he's watchin' us.'

The distant horseman was motionless, staring back across intervening country-side, and the backs of cattle, at Osborne and Baker. They started in his direction. The rider turned abruptly and loped eastward. Neither Snowy nor Bert mentioned it, but the horseman was clearly going to find some other men. Bert said, 'There ought to be a wagon-camp.'

But they did not find it, and in fact they did not make an effort to find it, because as they rode at a leisurely gait among the cattle, every one of which was shy enough of horsemen to spook a little, they saw three riders coming towards them from the east.

Snowy sneaked a hand down to pull

loose the tie-down thong on his Colt as he watched the oncoming men, who were riding bunched up and in no haste, their attention fixed upon Bert and Snowy. When they were close enough to be made out in detail Snowy said, 'They been on the road a spell.'

The rangemen were lean and weathered, their clothing was faded, none too clean, and each man rode with a booted carbine slung under a saddle-fender, something working range-riders rarely did.

When the riders were close enough they halted, did not speak, and flintily regarded Bert and Snowy. They were hostile, there was no doubt of that, and they also looked capable and ready.

Bert nodded a little as he said, 'Passin' through, gents?'

One of the strangers, a wide-shouldered, raw-boned man wearing a disreputable old black hat and a shirt with both elbows out, fixed Bert with hard blue eyes and answered curtly. 'You got an interest, mister?'

Bert's temper slipped a notch. 'Yeah, sort of an interest. We work for the feller who owns this range down here.'

A younger, roan-haired man made a gesture. 'Where are his cattle? Don't look to me like it's owned land. Where's the home-place?'

Bert jerked a thumb. 'Back yonder in the foothills a few miles. Yeah, it's deeded land.' He turned back toward the raw-boned man. 'Grazin' through, *amigo?*'

The raw-boned man rested two gloved hands atop the saddlehorn as he studied Bert, then Snowy, and looked back at Bert to say, 'We might be grazin' through. Did you come along to make sure we keep moving?'

'No,' stated Bert, 'we came down to see who you were.'

'I'm Wesley Moran,' stated the hard-faced, raw-boned man. 'And we're figurin' on lyin' over here for a few days. We got some tender-footed critters and they're all leg-weary. We been on the trail a hell of a spell.'

'You goin' on west through the mountains?' Bert asked, and this time the answer was tardier in arriving, and when he offered it Wesley Moran showed a hint of a bleak smile.

'We're grazin' off grass as we go, mister. Where we find good feed we lie over to rest the livestock. Unless of course the fellers who control a place ask us to push along...But this time we're not in the mood for pushin' along. Not as long as there's good feed.'

The hard-faced man had offered a challenge. Bert sat a moment considering it. During this interval the strangers sat waiting. Finally Snowy said, 'Let's go, Bert,' and he started to rein around. One of the three strangers snickered. He was a bull-necked, tow-headed youth aged no more than twenty. He had a nose which had been broken and which had healed with a slight right-twist to it.

When Bert, who had raised his rein-hand, heard the snicker he swung a look at the youth, and at once got his second challenge, but this time it was physical. The tow-headed rangeman swung gracefully to the ground, looking directly at Bert, waiting.

The raw-boned man named Wesley Moran spoke quietly to Bert. 'You better do like your partner says—just ride on off.'

Snowy reined back to face them, and Bert dropped a long look upon the waiting youth, then methodically dismounted and held out one rein to Snowy, but this was something Snowy Baker had no intention of buying into so he said it again. 'Bert, leave it be. Let's go.'

The tow-headed youth shifted his attention briefly to Snowy Baker, who was more nearly his bull-necked build but who was not quite as thick and was certainly much older, and without speaking, the youth spat, curled his mouth in contempt, and would have swung back over saddle-leather except that Bert said, 'You quitting?'

The youth whirled, no longer smiling or sneering, his blue eyes smoky. He dropped the reins and started forward.

Bert moved slightly to be away from his horse and when the oncoming rangeman halted suddenly ten feet off, Bert smiled, both arms at his side, both knees slightly sprung.

Wesley Moran spoke a trifle sharply to the youth. 'Another time, Dave. Get on your horse.'

The youth was hunched for the attack. For several moments his rock-steady stare remained upon Bert, then he loosened, made that contemptuous look again, turned on his heel and walked to his mount.

The three of them reined around and walked their horses back the way they had come, leaving Snowy with one hand on his sixgun butt, his mouth pulled flat, his gaze flintily upon their backs. As Bert remounted, Snowy said, 'Free-grazers,' then hauled his horse around to ride back in the direction from which he and Bert had come.

They went a half-mile before Bert said anything. 'Good thing Mister Northfield don't have any need for the feed down here.'

Snowy muttered something and rode the balance of the way back to their camp on the landswell in silence. As they were dismounting to strike camp, though, he said, 'No sense in you staying down here. There are no Mexican hat cattle around. Like I told you, there haven't been in a 'coon's age.'

Bert was tying his blanketroll aft of the cantle when he said, 'What are you goin' to do? Even if there were any horses, those fellers'll be after them.'

Snowy buckled his saddlebags closed, then tested the bedroll lashings, and leaned on his patient-standing horse as he gazed back down where they'd had their encounter. 'Darned if I know. I guess we could ride back and talk to old Amos. But I don't think that'll do any good either.' As he mounted, Snowy also said, 'Hell, it's not the grass. Northfield'll never use it.'

They angled off the landswell, riding more west than north, passing through more of those undulating rolling thick ribs of land which may have been formed millennia before by the surging undertow of a prehistoric sea, and which served as the foothill country to the distant northward mountains, except that they were really too far south to actually constitute foothills.

Northfield's ranch was in a very broad, wide, grassy swale and was not visible from the south, and was visible from the north only, provided someone was riding down from the direction of the rugged mountains. Otherwise, the wide valley was open to the east and west.

The buildings were of log, were old and grey-faded to match the flinty soil itself, except in the broad swale where, oddly enough, the earth was pure loam. Grass grew over an area of about four or five hundred acres as tall and strong as grass which grew in a better textured kind of earth elsewhere.

Amos Northfield's house was large, but the old man only lived in two rooms of it. The other parts had been closed off for many years, since his wife had died. The barn was low-roofed, more actually a horse barn than an equipment or cattle structure. There was no loft, for a very elemental reason; in the blue sage country winters were always mild, perhaps because it was high desert, possibly because for many miles around

31

the Northfield place great buttressing mountains sheltered the lower plain. No one put up hay for a hundred miles to the south, the east and west, not even for saddle-stock. No one built hay lofts into their barns, because there was no need to store feed.

There were horses across the valley, hock-deep in rich feed, and as Bert came down off the south slope, which was low and very gradual, he commented to Snowy about something he had shaken his head about when he had first ridden into the Northfield yard.

'Those horses'll get foundered, sure as hell, doin' nothing but eating out there.'

Snowy was watching the buildings, the main-house, the front of the barn, the little sheds for wagons, for shoeing, for smoking meat, for sheltering the shallow dug-well which supplied abundant water for domestic needs. His answer about the overweight horses was laconic.

'Try tellin' Mister Northfield that. I'll bet that since his wife died, nobody's told the old cuss anything. He's about as pigheaded as they come, even about little things that don't amount to a damn.'

Bert turned. 'Why do you work around him if you don't like him?'

'I like him,' exclaimed Snowy, reining around the foremost outbuilding into the yard. 'I can like folks and not be blind to their faults. You'll learn—if you stay around.'

They dismounted at the rack out front of the barn and Bert mentioned another thing which had impressed him the first time he'd ridden in. 'In a place like this a man'd ought to have a dog; if I lived here I'd have two or three dogs.'

Snowy said, 'If you lived out here all alone, and was as old as Mister Northfield, you'd deserve to have your head examined for not movin' into some town.'

They struck out across the yard toward the old log residence, and from a half-mile out a horse whinnied shrilly and Bert turned to look. The horse was looking towards the yard. It had seen the tethered horses, perhaps; it surely had not picked up their scent so soon.

CHAPTER 3

A SURPRISE

Possibly, as Snowy Baker had implied, Amos Northfield had been riding with one foot out of the stirrup for the last few years, but when he came down into the yard in a long-strided stalking gait he did not look senile, he looked irritable, even a little truculent.

He was a tall old man, thick-bodied and large-boned. He had an unshorn head of grey-white hair, hands the size of small hams, and a lined, deeply scored face which still retained the red-ruddy look of lifelong exposure.

He wore a shellbelt and holstered

Colt, old boots which had half the toes scuffed off, and a shirt and trousers which while having been laundered had probably never been ironed.

He glanced briefly at Snowy, then spoke to Bert Osborne. 'You found cattle already?'

He didn't address Bert as much as he hurled words at him. He had seemed gruff to Bert before, when he had hired Bert, but not this gruff or irritable, so Bert answered in a placating way.

'No, sir, but we came on to a big bunch of road-branded cattle down there. Maybe a thousand head.'

Old Amos stared, then slowly turned. 'Snowy?'

'The old brand isn't one I ever saw before, Mister Northfield, and the road-brand's nothin' but a letter M. I guess it stands for Moran. One of those fellers is named Wesley Moran.'

Northfield stepped into barn-shade before speaking again. 'I'll hitch up in the morning and we'll run them off.'

Snowy got a pained look on his face. 'Mister Northfield, I don't think they'll run worth a damn. Bert and I talked to them, and they wanted to fight us. Said they'd move on when the feed was gone.'

'How many?' growled the big old man.

'Three.'

Northfield's head dropped a little, his deepset eyes glowed at Snowy. 'Three! Only three and you fellers tucked tail and ran?'

Bert interrupted. 'We didn't tuck tail. We came back to find out if you had maybe given someone the right to graze across you. And to tell you what we saw down there.'

Amos Northfield glanced once toward his residence, then stepped up to lean across the tie-rack and squint eastward up his long, grassy valley, silent for a while. Eventually he let go a rattling big breath and spoke in a less disagreeable tone.

'How long'll they be out there?'

Bert and Snowy exchanged a glance; suddenly the fire had gone out of the old man. Bert risked a guess. 'There is good feed down there. I'd guess haven't been any cattle on it for years. They could graze that off with a thousand head in maybe a month.'

'No,' the old man said, 'they got to be gone before a month.'

Again Snowy and Bert exchanged a glance. Bert tried something. 'Well, we could go back and tell 'em they can stay a couple of weeks.'

Northfield thought about that for a long while and finally nodded his head very slowly. 'No more than two weeks.'

'If,' said Bert, 'they'll go in two weeks, and leave a lot of good feed behind.'

Northfield straightened up off the tie-rack. 'They'll go in two weeks—or they'll never cover another mile...You fellers bed down in the bunkhouse. I'll be down after a spell and have supper with you.'

Northfield turned and walked back the same way he had walked down there, with that long-strided stalking gait of his. Snowy waited until the door slammed, then said, 'Now you tell me he don't have a few marbles missing.'

They put up their horses, and after Bert returned from the corral he found Snowy leaning on a stall door, looking in at a leggy, big, handsome gelding, obviously with a lot of thoroughbred breeding behind him. Snowy said, 'You know what I think? I think the old man's got someone at the house with him. I never saw this horse before; the old man don't have anything on the ranch bred-up like this animal.' Snowy turned toward Bert, but the taller and younger man saw nothing strange in Snowy's remark, so he shrugged and said he was going to wash up.

The bunkhouse was like the cook-house and most of the other buildings; it smelled stale, had layers of dust every-where, obviously had not been inhabited in years, and the most recent initial carved on the log walls which had a date under it had been made twenty years earlier.

A few riders from back in those days had carved their full names with the dates. One name "Rattlesnake Rowe" was directly behind the wood-stove under a shelf of ancient cups and plates. It had no date, just the words "still riding", directly beneath the name. Bert paused to briefly wonder if Rattlesnake *was* still riding, then he dumped his bedroll upon a rope-sprung wall-bunk and draped both saddlebags from a wall-peg before going in search of the basin and bucket so he could clean up.

When Snowy came in later he was thoughtful and quiet. He used the leaky basin Bert had found in the well-house, and most of the water Bert had brought to the rack along the bunkhouse ball-wall. When he came inside Bert had the wood-stove fired up. The smell of ancient dust and rusty stovepipe inspired Snowy to go open the front door. The meal Bert prepared was meagre, consisting of leftovers from their meal this morning down near the sagebrush plain, and looked like clinkers from a shoeing forge when he divided it among three tin plates, then filled three cups with black coffee, and sat down to roll a smoke while they awaited the arrival of Amos Northfield.

As he smoked, Bert made an observation. 'There's something about this place,' he murmured. 'When I hired on I didn't stay here. Maybe if I had...'

Snowy stood in the open doorway, looking out where night was settling, and where the only light except for the lantern Bert had found and fired up in the bunkhouse, was over in the main-house, and it looked about as feeble as the one behind Snowy's back. Snowy said, 'This place always sort of gave me the creeps. Even back some years when the old man kept a couple of steady riders. One of those fellers called it "melancholy". "Real melancholy", and I guess that's what it is.' Snowy turned. 'He's nutty as a peach-orchard boar.'

They heard Amos coming; that stride of his was unique enough to be distinctive anywhere. When he walked in with a slow nod, Snowy closed the door and Bert pointed to one of the tin plates, and Amos sat down. He was hatless with his mane of unshorn nearly white hair slightly askew. He had a preoccupied air as he reached for a coffee-cup and said, 'I changed my mind. For the next few days you boys can stay here.'

He offered no explanation and attacked his meal while Bert and Snowy did the same. Amos eventually raised his head, chewing methodically on a tough piece of meat. 'You'll eat better,' he exclaimed, and went back to his meal until Snowy mentioned something that was bothering him a little, now.

'Amos, I can lie around for a few days, but no more'n that.'

The shaggy brows lifted a little. 'If they got cattle and men down there, you're not goin' to locate any mustangs.'

Snowy persisted. 'Yeah, I know. But I still got to make a living.'

'Then,' stated the big old man, 'I'll hire you on full time at regular wages.'

Snowy drained his cup and went to refill it as he answered. 'You don't need two men. You don't have that many cattle.'

Northfield swallowed the last piece of refried meat with a visible effort, drained his cup and held it out. 'While you're up,' he said, and was silent until

Snowy had poured the cup full. 'I don't need anyone to tell me what I need and don't need, Snowy, and you need steady work. All right; for a few weeks then, and if you still got a hankering to run wild horses, you can quit.' The old man sipped the coffee, which was too hot, and put the cup aside as he turned his sunk-set eyes upon Bert Osborne, who had been silently busy eating. He suddenly said, 'You ever been a lawman?' And Bert blinked in surprise. 'No.'

The old man continued to regard Bert. 'You ever been on the outside of the law?'

Snowy returned to his seat, darkly scowling. Old Amos was committing an inexcusable breach of range-country etiquette; personal questions was unpardonable. They could also lead to unpleasant consequences.

Bert said, 'No,' again, and studied the old man's craggy features, not as much annoyed as astonished. Those oldtimers in particular rigidly observed range etiquette.

Northfield looked at Snowy, saw his black look, and shoved his plate away, brought the cup in closer and sat hunched with both hands around it. He seemed to be addressing Snowy Baker next.

'I got some trouble, gents. Until this morning I figured I'd be able to handle it alone. Then you boys rode in, and since then I been thinkin' different.' Old Amos took a swallow of bitter coffee, then seemed to brace himself for something he did not want to do. 'You saw the horse in the barn?'

Snowy did not nod, he raised his face slowly, as though with a sudden premonition. 'Yeah, we saw it. Breedy big black horse.'

Northfield cleared his throat and dropped his eyes to the cup's contents. 'I got a hurt feller over at the house, and yesterday he wasn't real bad, but this mornin' he taken a turn for the worse— and now he's out of his head about half the time.' The sunk-set eyes swept up swiftly. 'Trouble is, even with my glasses I can't see well enough.'

Bert was puzzled. 'Well enough for what, Mister Northfield?'

'Well, boys, he's got to be cut on, and I dassn't do it.'

Snowy was staring at the old man. 'Spit it out,' he said curtly. 'What ails this feller?'

'He's got a bullet in him, boys.'

Bert and Snowy stared. Amos Northfield dropped his glance to the cup's contents again. After a while Snowy Baker spoke. 'How did he get this bullet in him, Amos? Damn it; this is worse'n pullin' teeth. Who is this feller?'

'Well, boys, I knew him a few years back.'

Bert said, 'Is he an outlaw?'

Amos fidgeted. 'Yes.'

Bert began putting it together. 'He got shot and he came riding down here, and you knew him so you took him in?'

'Yes,' stated the old man, finally raising his face. 'I don't know where or how he got shot. He was too sick to talk and he sure as hell isn't in any shape to talk now. I can tell you this much about him from years back—he's a hell of a rangeman. He's as good a feller with livestock as you'll ever come across.'

Snowy arose from the table. 'What in the hell,' he exclaimed, scowling at Northfield. 'Why in hell did you wait all day to say anything?'

'I wasn't worried about you, Snowy. You aren't a kid about things like this—but Bert here, I had my doubts. I didn't ask him about himself when I hired him on.'

Snowy stepped from the table, then reached for the lantern as he briskly said, 'Let's go look at this feller. We'll worry about other things afterwards.'

As Amos and Bert arose, Snowy stood at the doorway, wagging his head.

They hiked to the main-house and it was as dingy and musty as Bert had thought it might be. Once, though, the curtains had been clean, the mantle had been polished, and where old Amos had worn a dustless path from his unkempt kitchen across the parlour to the front door, the entire floor had been dustless.

The bedroom Amos took them to also had a smoking lamp in it with a dirty mantle. Snowy put the lantern beside it, which helped a little.

The man in the bed was partially undressed. He was a husky individual with a flushed face, perspiration on his upper lip and forehead, and although his eyes were open, the pupils were so dilated Bert thought his eyes were dark, when in fact they were actually light coloured. The man had strawberry-roan hair, which was neither blond nor red, and he needed both a shearing and a shave.

Snowy leaned and looked, then straightened back to lift the crude and cumbersome bandage Amos had wound round the stranger's middle. Bert held the lamp aloft so that Snowy could see under the bandaging, and when Snowy sighed, Bert had a sinking feeling, but Snowy straightened up briskly. 'First, someone's got to clean the mantles on those lights,' he said. 'And be sure they got a full bowl of oil in 'em.' He regarded Bert as though Amos were not there. 'Do you puke or faint around blood?' he asked.

Bert shook his head and let his gaze wander to the unconscious stranger. 'How bad is it?'

'Bad enough,' stated Snowy Baker. 'But if it'd been got to yesterday or the day before it wouldn't be too bad.' Having delivered himself of that ambiguous answer he said, 'Stay here with him, Amos. Bert, come along to the kitchen with me, and fetch those lamps.'

Bert obeyed, leaving Amos back there in a dark room with his outlaw friend. In the kitchen they hunted for a coal-oil can and Bert filled each lamp separately so that Snowy would have light while he set a pail of water to heat on the wood-stove. Snowy rummaged for clean towels, found none and went through from the kitchen into a bedroom and returned with two of Northfield's clean shirts. He seemed to know what he was doing, but when Bert had both the lamp mantles cleaned and the brightness had been increased at least ten times, Snowy looked at the younger man with a quizzical expression as he said, 'You ever dig a bullet out of anyone?'

Bert hadn't. 'No. Have you?'

Snowy shook his head. 'Out of a horse once, but never a man.'

'But you're goin' to try it?'

Snowy gazed straight at Bert. 'You know what lead poisonin' is?'

'Yeah.'

'Well, Bert, the bullet comes out or the feller dies, and dyin' from poisonin' is a hell of a way to go. That's what it amounts to. We get it out of him, or he dies a hell of a death, and if I botch it he's goin' to die too, but at least it'll be over a lot quicker.' Snowy continued to gaze at the taller and younger man. 'Ain't that the damndest gamble you ever heard of?'

It was for a fact and Bert went to a half-empty bottle of whiskey on the sink and took two swallows, then offered Snowy the bottle but Snowy only took one swallow, and a small one at that.

'Bring the lamps,' he said, holding the bottle to take it along also. 'When the water's real hot you can fetch the bucket in there. I got to whet my knife.'

Bert picked up the lantern and the lamp and followed Snowy back to the bedroom.

CHAPTER 4

A PAIR OF WOLVES

Snowy worked for an hour, then took another swallow from the whiskey bottle and told Amos to wipe blood off the outlaw's side so he could see what he was doing. He also told Bert to hold the lamp lower.

When he dropped the slug on to a bedside table with a marble top it sounded very loud in the quiet room. Snowy had sweat down the front and back of his shirt and although the whiskey helped, Snowy was using up energy and spirit a lot faster than any amount of whiskey could have supplied it.

He got Bert to help, finally after he had thoroughly cleansed the wound with hot water. They got a better and smaller bandage made of Amos Northfield's shirt. The other shirt they had cut into strips to sop up blood with.

Bert finally put the lamp upon the marble-topped table and flexed an arm which ached from holding the thing up for so long.

Amos took a long pull on the whiskey bottle and stood gazing at the ashen-faced outlaw. 'If poisonin' has already set in...' he murmured, and continued to stand in deep silence.

Snowy left the room to wash his hands and arms. In his absence Bert spoke his mind. 'Whether your friend lives or dies, Mister Northfield, Snowy did a hell of a job.'

Old Northfield nodded without looking away from the inert outlaw.

'Snowy's a hell of a good man. He's highly thought of in the territory.' For a moment the old man continued to stand there, slightly bowed and very solemn, then he said, 'There'll likely be a reward on this feller, Bert—if you're money-hungry,' and before Bert could reply to that, Northfield had something else to say, and this time his words had more significance for Osborne.

'Whoever shot him most likely knows he hit him, and that could mean there'll be someone ride into the yard directly. I kept watch yesterday, but maybe Rattlesnake come a hell of a distance, and for a fact he's plenty *coyote*; if he had his wits while he was gettin' away from them, he'd know a lot of ways to shade his tracks. But if they come...' Amos looked around slowly.

Bert understood, or thought he understood, what was in the old man's mind, but he did not speak, and moments later, when Snowy returned with his sleeves down again and buttoned, there was no need to speak. Just one thing stuck in Bert's mind. The name Rattlesnake. He had seen it carved into the bunkhouse wall that afternoon. He looked at the unconscious man, who was breathing in a shallow and fluttery way, and thought that Rattlesnake should look a lot older than he was, if he had carved his name over yonder as far back as most of those other men had.

Snowy scattered Bert's thoughts by saying, 'Mister Northfield, I wouldn't give a plugged *centavo* for that feller's chances, but, win or lose, if someone was mad enough at him to shoot him, then someone will sure as hell still be lookin' for him—and this is the only set of buildings for a hell of a long ride in any direction.'

Snowy did not say more, he did not have to. Northfield went to a chair and sank down. 'I know all that,' he replied. 'That's why I said you boys had ought to stay on the place for a few days.'

Snowy had evidently done quite a bit of thinking out there in the kitchen because he came right back at the old man. 'I got no reason to buck the law, especially over a man I never saw before. Bert don't either.'

Northfield settled tiredly into the chair and gazed at the pair of younger men. 'Let's wait and see. Maybe no one'll show up. You want to turn his black horse out with my stock?'

Snowy nodded and led Bert back out upon the veranda, where they were both surprised at the low position of the half moon. Daylight was not far off. As they walked slowly through pre-dawn chill in the direction of the bunkhouse, Bert ordered his thoughts enough to say, 'He's no more crazy than I am. And I'll tell you what I think: in a man's lifetime he won't find more'n maybe one or two friends who'd do for him what old Northfield has done for that feller.'

They were inside the dark bunkhouse before Snowy heaved a rattling sigh, sank down on his bedroll and said, 'I'm too damned tired to sleep, an' we got no light or I'd play you a few hands of blackjack.'

Bert was not too tired to sleep. He kicked out of his boots across the room, shed his hat and sat down, thinking back. 'How did you have the guts to do that, Snowy?'

The answer from the darkness was frank. 'I didn't have. That meat we had for supper was goin' up an' down like a monkey on a rope. The whiskey helped, but, most of all, it had to be done...But I'll buy you a new hat if that feller's alive this time tomorrow.'

Snowy lay back fully clothed and stared upwards into the darkness, while upon the opposite side of the room Bert got into his soogans, closed his eyes, and within ten seconds was snoring.

Daylight came early to the high desert

country, except in wintertime, and when Bert went down to look after the horses something very distant and moving caught his attention from the east. For a moment he got a tight feeling in the chest, then it left and he stood in the barn opening, looking, and waiting. But if that tiny distant object had been a mounted man, it turned off a considerable distance from the Northfield meadow and probably went southward, although Bert did not see it do that; all he knew was the moving object went behind a landswell and did not emerge, so it either stopped back there or had turned southward.

Snowy called across the yard, and Bert finished inside the barn then trudged in the direction of the bunkhouse, but Snowy said old Amos had said for them to come to the main-house for breakfast. As they walked out into the coolness of late dawn Snowy said, 'He's goin' to tell us his friend died last night.'

But Snowy was wrong. Old North-field met them at the door and with nothing more than a nod led the way to his dingy kitchen, where he had fried both meat and potatoes, and had a platter of tortillas in the place of bread or toast to go with their black coffee.

As they sat down he said, 'You lose your bet,' to Snowy, and shoved the platter of meat toward the younger man. 'He's still alive.'

For a while they ate without con-versing. What the old man had said last night at supper in the bunkhouse was true; they would eat better if they remained at the ranch. He not only had more food but, surprisingly enough, he made very good coffee.

Bert got the pleats out of his gut and considered the old man. He was curious about the helpless man in the back bed-room, but would not ask questions.

He told them about seeing something, a mounted man, perhaps, or a large animal, miles out. Northfield listened with his knife and fork poised, but Snowy went right on eating. 'One of those free-grazers,' he suggested. 'They'd scout up the ranch after their run-in with us yesterday.'

He was probably right. Northfield did not agree nor disagree, he refilled all three cups and asked if Snowy had turned the black horse out. Snowy hadn't, not in the night, but said he would do it this morning. He also said that he and Bert ought to go north and hunt cattle today. Amos did not disagree with that, in fact he said nothing at all until they had finished their coffee and were arising, then he growled something about visiting the wounded outlaw and led the way.

The room had clean sunlight streaming in a window, which made it look less like something out of a nightmare, which was the way it had seemed to Bert last night. There was an earthen crock on the floor near the bed with a corn-cob stopper in it. The smell of whiskey was noticeable.

The wounded man's face was flushed and sweaty. He needed a shave more than ever this morning. His breathing was deeper, which Bert thought was probably encouraging, and he looked up at them with eyes which seemed to focus, which he had not done before, but Bert thought the gaze was glassy and rather fixed.

Northfield said, 'Weak as a kitten.'

Snowy stepped over to lift the blankets and peer at the bandage, lowered the blankets gently and smiled at the outlaw. He was looking at the outlaw but he spoke to Northfield. 'He's better, but be damned if I know why.'

They left the room and went out to the veranda, where morning heat was beginning to build a little. Northfield said, 'Stay in the clear, and come on back early,' then he returned to the house.

They took the breedy black gelding on a shank and led him out a mile or so where the Mexican Hat horses stood like statues, watching their approach, and when they freed the gelding the other horses began their ritual faunching and pawing as they warily sidled around to sniff him. In any band there were always a few horses who wanted to challenge a newcomer, but excepting stallions and ridglings, or maybe a horsing, cranky mare or two they were not fighters, provided the newcomer stood his ground, but if he ran, then the whole band would be after him, which was why Snowy had not wanted to turn the black horse out last night, in a country where he did not know where the pitfalls were.

They sat their saddles for a while, watching. The black horse was calm. He had evidently been through this many times, because until a stud-necked buckskin reached out to nip, he did not move. The moment the buckskin's teeth touched his rump, though, the black lashed out. Two shod hooves bounding off a rib-cage sounded like a drumroll. The buckskin whirled and fled, the other horses did not go any closer, and the black horse dropped his head to start cropping grass.

It was not over yet, but at least now that the other horses knew the black horse would fight back, they would be a little more respectful.

Snowy and Bert headed north-east, in the direction Snowy said they would probably find the old man's critters. As they rode along, Snowy said, 'Old Amos's got his friend primed with corn whisky, but you can't keep a sick man like that for ever.'

Bert was studying the flow of land. 'He sure looked a lot better.'

'The whiskey,' stated Snowy, and finally also lifted his head to look for signs of movement. 'If that feller don't get an infection I'll be surprised as hell.' He raised a gloved hand to point. There were cattle to the west of them. They changed course to ride at a steady walk in that direction.

The country north of the home-place was rugged without being precipitously so; if there were cliffs up there—called *barrancas* in New Mexico's blue sage country—they were a considerable distance off, perhaps closer to the far timber-tiered mountains.

Where the Northfield cattle were grazing along, the ground was rough and crumbly, tan stone and a surprising amount of good grass. Snowy led the way among the cattle, as close as mounted men could get, then showed the Northfield brand to Bert.

There were three horned bulls, old and scarred and willing to challenge the riders, but the cows gave ground even though the horsemen did not crowd them. Bert thought the calf crop looked good. Snowy agreed. They then spent two hours making a rough count, and during the course of a big sashay westward they found a pair of big dog-wolves slinking along in a deep arroyo. The wolves did not see either horseman. They were intent upon stalking an old cow with a baby calf which was several hundred yards from the nearest cattle.

Without speaking, Bert and Snowy pulled back from the edge of the arroyo, turned southerly at a quiet walk so as not to send reverberations through the ground, and went steadily down nearer the old cow. She watched their approach with her head close to the ground, shiny big curved horns menacingly low. She did not bolt, probably because of her curled up baby calf sleeping under a sage clump, his belly full of warm milk.

Bert dismounted and drew his Colt. Snowy did the same. They used the Indian trick of remaining upon the off-side of their horses so that when the wolves surfaced up out of the arroyo they would not see mounted men, just a pair of horses.

The old cow, veteran of many winters and probably just as many encounters with predators, suddenly picked up a scent and shifted her stance. She was watching the lip of the arroyo now.

Both wolves came up at the same time. One halted suddenly, testing the air. He had caught man-scent. The other wolf was concentrating on just one thing —that sleeping baby calf. He started forward.

Snowy shot the wolf who was testing the air. He went backwards down into the arroyo in a threshing heap of grey fur. The other wolf had probably never been shot at before; he made the fatal mistake of stopping dead-still for two seconds, searching the area for the source of that gunshot. An old wolf never would have done that, he would have whirled instantly and fled.

Bert killed the second wolf with a shot that put him down without a struggle.

The old cow bellowed in distress, alerting every other critter within hearing distance. They all came to her aid in a lumbering rush as she hurried to stand above her calf.

Snowy and Bert got back astride and turned to lope northward. It was good sense to be wary of bulls, but the most dangerous animal in a herd of cattle was a cow with a helpless little calf. They rode out a half-mile, then halted to look back. Cattle were around the old cow, pawing, flinging dun dirt until it made a thin cloud above them, and the dead wolf got his share of hooking and trampling too.

The sun was off-centre. Bert rolled and lit a smoke and Snowy said they'd earned their pay today as they headed for home.

Midway along Bert looked at his companion. 'How come if you knew the old man's cattle were up here—he didn't know it?'

'I told you—he's a few bubbles shy, that's why.'

Bert smoked and thought for a while before speaking again. 'Naw; I got the feelin' there's more to it than that. Snowy, last night in the bedroom he was as natural as you or me...But sure as hell there is something wrong...'

Snowy grunted and kept riding.

CHAPTER 5

RIDDEN DOWN!

For three days both rangemen rode out every morning. They hunted predators, of which they only found one other—a gaunt old puma who had no business being out of the mountains, except that he was too old and slow to catch deer or antelope, and cattle were his last resource, other than rabbits and field-mice.

They killed him with carbines, but that was the last time they carried saddleguns, and it was also the last predator they encountered.

The cattle had shifted a few miles

more westerly, but it had clearly been an exceptional springtime, plenty of warm rains without frosty nights, and there was grass everywhere. Northfield had two salt-licks, one up where they had killed the brace of wolves and the second one about four miles to the west. It was towards the second lick that the cattle were now gravitating and as long as there was good feed over there to go with the salt, as well as a creek, the critters would not drift much for a while.

They had been eating at the bunk-house, living out of it, and except for a few brief encounters with Amos Northfield, had left the yard early and had returned late.

Northfield told them the outlaw was still hanging on, and Snowy grunted about that, still very sceptical of Rattle-snake's chances, but the late afternoon of the fourth day, when they were off-saddling in the barn, Northfield came down to invite them up for supper, and during the course of some casual conversation he told them Rattlesnake was drinking beef tea like it was going out of style.

After Northfield left the barn, Snowy said, 'Likely got such a danged fever he'd drink anything.'

But after they had cleaned up and crossed the yard Amos took them to the back bedroom, where the wounded outlaw met them with a weak smile. Amos introduced them around. Rattlesnake said, 'I'm powerful obliged to you fellers. I sure as hell wouldn't have made it without you.'

Snowy could not resist. 'Mister Rowe, you ain't out of the woods yet.'

Bert thought that was an unnecessary thing to say so he spoke encouragingly. 'You sure got good colour. You must have the constitution of a horse. You look like maybe you'll be up and around in another week or so.'

Amos took them to the kitchen, poured three water-tumblers full of water and whiskey, handed two of them to his riders and took the third glass to the popping old wood-stove, where he had been frying spuds and steak. He said, 'How are the cattle?'

They told him about the puma, about the general condition of the animals, and sat at the table, sipping. He said, 'We got scouted up this afternoon,' and went on working with his iron skillets as though neither of his riders were staring at him. 'Couple of fellers, from the tracks.'

Bert was not particularly interested in tracks. 'Did you see 'em; get a good look at 'em?'

'Not a good look, no. By the time I saw the tracks they were already headin' south. From a distance I'd say they were maybe those free-grazers you fellers met last week.'

Snowy finished his drink and put the

glass aside. 'You hope it was them,' he exclaimed a trifle dourly. 'Because if it warn't, why then Mister Rowe's friends are lookin' for him.'

Amos brought the platter of boot-leather meat and went back for the big bowl of fried potatoes. Later, as he was filling the coffee-cups he had an observation to make.

'If the cattle are settled, you boys might ride south a little in the morning and see where those trespassing sons of bitches are.' Bert was hungry. He had little to say anyway, so he concentrated on eating. So did Snowy, until he was about two-thirds full and was reaching for his cup of java, then he said, 'The trouble with free-grazers—at least in my experience—is that if folks don't stand up to them they fan out and never move on.'

Amos surprised both his hired riders by saying, 'Well, what the hell, since I don't need the feed, haven't put any stock down there in years, they might as well graze it down. It'll make for better grass next season.'

After supper when Snowy and Bert were out back at the corrals having a smoke and watching the horses, the older rider wagged his head. 'Last week he jumped square in the middle of us for not chousin' those free-grazers off his land. Tonight, he's as washy as a scourin' calf. And you don't think his mind's slippin' its cogs.'

Bert did not pursue this because every time he did they had an argument. He continued to lean and smoke, and idly watch the horses, but if every man who changed his mind was senile, then the world was full of 'em, and most of 'em weren't old, either.

They played a few hands of blackjack before retiring. Bert won twenty-four cents, which sent Snowy to bed in a bleak mood. In the morning, though, he had recovered. They rode south with a great orange ball beginning to edge up along the distant curve of crusty high-desert country, got down there, to the identical place where they had first seen strange cattle, in mid-morning and had to trail west a couple of miles to see cattle.

Evidently down here, too, there was so much feed grazing livestock moved slowly and sluggishly. They rode out into the open country to have a closer look at the road-branded animals. Snowy kept his head moving. They had seen no herders but they were down there, somewhere. He also searched for a canvas-topped wagon; free-grazers usually had such a rig along because, unlike ordinary drovers, who herded a drive to a destination, then left it there, free-grazers had no real destination. They lived out of a wagon and drove their cattle anywhere there was feed. When the herd was fat enough and they were close to corrals at some town where the railroad passed through, they sold off. Sometimes they grazed off other people's grass for a couple of years before shipping out.

But there was no wagon in sight, which puzzled Snowy, but he said nothing about it as he and Bert Osborne got close enough to read brands and consider the condition of the animals. They saw a few foot-sore cattle but not very many. They also saw quite a number of big two- and three-year-old steers which were in good shape; not prime shape but good enough to sell. And there were sassy calves everywhere.

What they did not see was a pair of horsemen circling far out and around, then coming down-country behind them. They did not hear them either because of the noise the cattle were making.

The first inkling that they were not alone down there was when a rock struck Bert's horse in the rump. The horse gave a tremendous bound ahead, Bert nearly went off. Only his five-inch cantle made it possible for him to stay up there and fight the startled horse around.

The two men were laughing as they sat a dozen or so yards away. It was the tow-headed, bull-necked youth and the old man Wesley Moran had not named, but Snowy and Bert remembered Dave, the tow-head.

Bert's surprise turned to white anger in a flash. He rode directly at the pair of free-grazers, their smiles faded and they started to rein clear but Snowy called ahead in a snarl.

He had his sixgun above the saddle-swells, cocked and stone-steady. The free-grazers had let their contempt get them into a bad situation. Neither man had made a move towards his hip-holster and now it was too late.

Bert came up on the right side of the tow-headed youth and lashed out. The blow did not do any damage but it connected, and all three of the men discovered something at the same time; Bert Osborne could strike so fast it was hard to see the fist coming.

Dave went down off the near-side of his horse and Bert whirled, barrelled into Dave's animal, shouldered on past it and dug in the spurs. Dave had almost no time to evade being ridden down, but he tried. He hurled himself sideways, struck the ground, rolled and bounced to his feet to run. His companion yelled to him.

'Draw! Draw damn it!'

Dave tried, but it was difficult when he was running as hard as he could with a charging horse less than two yards to the rear. He got the gun out and twisted to fire it, but he lost yardage and Bert's horse struck him head on. Dave went down in a heap, lost his sixgun, and struggled in a dazed way to get up on to all fours.

Bert hit the ground on both feet fifteen feet distant and went back. He saw Dave blinking up at him, and paused, giving the youth time to stand up. Dave made a good effort, got upright but could not clear his head and stood there with both arms hanging at his sides.

Snowy and the other free-grazer held their breath, full attention riveted upon what they both expected to be a massacre.

Bert stood poised for a long time, face white with anger, his stare unblinkingly fixed on the tow-headed rangeman. Then he stepped past, scooped up Dave's gun, methodically shucked out the loads and sank the useless gun into Dave's holster and turned his back to remount his Mexican Hat horse.

Dave spat dust and dirt as Bert rode past him back to where the other free-grazer was sitting like a statue, Snowy Baker's cocked Colt still effectively neutralising him.

When Bert reined up they stared at one another before Bert said, 'Get down, you son of a bitch!'

The free-grazer calmly looped his reins and leaned to dismount, but Snowy interrupted. 'Bert, leave it be.' Then he asked the free-grazer his name and the older man eased back slightly in the saddle ignoring Bert and looking at Snowy.

'Wood Kendall,' he said.

'Get your friend on his horse, Wood, and go find Mister Moran, and tell him to get his gawddamned cattle off Northfield range by day after tomorrow.'

Wood Kendall loosened a little, still eyeing Snowy, who was about his own age, and ignoring the younger man with the blazing eyes sitting ten feet distant, waiting. Wood Kendall was a calm individual. So far he had shown no agitation. He did not show any now as he said, 'Cowboy, you got some message for Wes Moran—you carry it to him.'

Bert gigged his horse until their legs rubbed. Wood Kendall had seen how fast Bert could strike and swung to watch as he also leaned far to the right side. But Bert did not attempt to hit the older man. He said, 'You'll carry the message to him.' He added nothing, made no threat, but there was no doubt at all about what was going to happen if Wood Kendall gave Bert the kind of an answer he had given Snowy Baker.

The older free-grazer kept his sun-bronzed, hard, lined face turned toward Bert over an interlude of silence, then as calmly as before he yielded. 'All right, mister. Just don't think what you boys says is goin' to carry a damned bit of weight with us.'

Kendall reined back and rode around, scooped up the reins to Dave's horse and led the beast over to where Dave had retrieved his hat and was waiting, still shaken but no longer dazed.

Snowy did not ease down the dog of his Colt or make any move to holster it as the pair of free-grazers got resettled in their saddles and rode easterly at a steady walk.

Then, when they were beyond hand-gun range, Snowy put up his gun. He was by nature as calm and usually as unexcitable as was Wood Kendall, but now he spat, thumbed back his hat and stared at Bert.

'You never give me no idea you were quick-tempered,' he said. 'I had no idea you was goin' after that damned fool.'

Bert used a soiled cuff to squeeze off sweat before replying. 'What was I supposed to do, make out like I thought it was funny, an' laugh with them too?'

Snowy dropped it, but clearly Bert Osborne was one of those men whose temper kept them irritable for a long time, because as he and Snowy were heading back, he said, 'Why did you tell 'em to get the cattle off our range by day after tomorrow? Mister Northfield said they could hang on for another couple of weeks.'

'Seemed like the right time Bert, since we had the whip hand,' stated Baker, 'And, besides, that's been sort of gnawin' on me—them just arriving and taking over, and darin' Mexican Hat to do anything about it.'

For another mile Bert was silent. In fact except to clear his pipes and expectorate, and to mutter something about Dave being a damned idiot, he did not speak until they were in the yard in late afternoon, where Bert could shed his hat and shirt and sluice off over at the stone trough near the shoeing-shed. Then he turned as Snowy slowly ambled over, and grinned.

'Thanks,' he said.

Snowy stepped into shed-shade. 'For what? If I hadn't thrown down on the other one they'd have cleaned both our ploughs. They still may do it, Bert. I don't know how much you been around men like that bunch, but I can tell you, once someone stirs 'em up—hail Columbia!'

Bert straightened up, reaching for his sweaty shirt. As he put it on he sighed and said, 'All I came down into this damned country for was to get a job.'

Snowy pondered on that briefly before replying to it. 'Boy, didn't your paw ever tell you about New Messico; not just down along the Mex border but back up here too? It's a mean, treacherous country. If rattlers don't get you, or Gila monsters, or them big furry damned poisonous spiders, why then renegades likely will, because down here we got a renegade for every clump of sagebrush. We're bound to have, this close to the Mex line. They come ridin' down from Montana, Wyoming, Colorado—every darned place you can think of where they robbed stages or banks or stole horses, or rustled cattle, killed people, or escaped from a jailhouse... You take that feller over in the house. I knew I'd heard that name somewhere. It only just came to me while we were ridin' back a while ago. There was a wanted poster on him over at Deming. I saw it a couple of years back. And up at Raton too.'

'What's he wanted for?'

'Horse-stealin' and bein' a fugitive from somewhere up north, seems like it was either Montana or Wyoming. They want him over in Nebraska too. If I recollect right, he hired on with the railroad until he knew all the schedules, then, by golly, he commenced stoppin' 'em in places no one would have thought of and blew up the strong boxes. Sort of like Jesse and Frank James, only this Rowe feller—he's as slippery as a snake.' Snowy paused and drew down a big breath, then changed the subject. 'Well, anyway, New Messico'll edcuate the hell out of you, Bert...if you keep alive.'

CHAPTER 6

AN UNFRIENDLY ACT

Amos Northfield listened to everything his rangeriders had to report concerning their fight with the free-grazers, then sat there on the front veranda, scowling blackly.

It was later, after supper with a big full moon riding majestically overhead and the three of them had time for calm reflection. Amos was silent for so long that Bert got uncomfortable, and the less sensitive Snowy Baker got disgusted and arose to head for the bunkhouse.

Then Northfield said, 'All right. What's done is done. Now then—do you expect they'll move on?'

Snowy gave an unequivocal reply. 'No.' Then he leaned on a porch upright, looking at the pair of seated men as he spoke again. 'But they'll sure want a piece of someone's hide for what happened today.'

'Stay away from there,' stated old Amos. 'Just let it simmer, and directly maybe they'll get along.'

This time, Bert was not straddling the fence when Snowy and old Amos disagreed. He was no longer angry about what had happened on the south range, but he *was* still indignant about it, so he said, 'Mister Northfield, stayin' away isn't goin' to do any good. We told 'em to move along. We can't go back on that.'

'Anyway,' stated Snowy dryly, 'their kind don't forget. They're very good at bushwhacking. That pale-headed son of a bitch Bert rode down—he's not goin' to let it go. Not in a million years.'

Old Northfield flared up at them. 'Why the hell didn't you just leave 'em be, like I said to do?'

Neither Bert nor Snowy spoke for a long time, then Bert also arose to stand near the three broad steps leading down off the veranda as he said, 'Mister Northfield...I quit.'

Northfield's head came up quickly. He stared at Bert Osborne with most of the angry scowl gone. 'Sure,' he stated. 'You get a range fight going, then you ride off an' leave me to handle it. I can't even set a saddle, and can't see to shoot any more.'

The bitterness in the old man's voice made Bert fidget a little. He temporised, conscious of the look he was getting from Snowy Baker. 'Well, damn it all, Mister Northfield, any place I ever worked the boss always backed up his men.'

Northfield seemed ready to say something about that, then looked away, down across the moonlit empty big yard and remained silent for so long that Bert and Snowy were ready to depart before he opened his mouth.

'Those goddamned free-grazers are right where they hadn't ought to be,' he said, and still did not look at the other two men. 'It's not the feed; I told you that last night. I haven't put cattle down there in fifteen years.'

Snowy glanced at Bert, but Osborne did not notice because he was gazing perplexedly at Amos Northfield.

Northfield struggled up out of his chair and stood like a big, bent bird in the roof-shadow. 'Go bed down,' he said, reverting to his usual gruff tone again. 'We'll talk in the morning. Good-night, gents.'

They left him and trudged towards the bunkhouse without exchanging a word until Snowy had the lantern lit. Then he turned and said, 'Well; *now* tell me he's not scrambled in the *cabeza*. He sent you down there the day we met to hunt for his cattle. I told you then, he hadn't had any cattle on the blue sage range since Hector was a pup.'

Bert sank down at the old table and flung his hat aside. 'Snowy,' he said softly, 'he's not senile. There's something else happenin' around here.'

'What,' exclaimed Baker, dropping down solidly across the table. 'Just tell me what.'

'He sent me down there...He hadn't forgot he had no cattle down there. Tonight he said it straight out. No cattle of his on the blue sage range for fifteen years. *For fifteen years*. Not the last few years, and not lately, or some other darned statement. *Fifteen years*. He knew to the year how long it had been. But he still sent me down there.'

'Aw, hell,' grumbled Snowy, twisting to kick out of his boots. 'He's crazy an' that's all there is—'

'Why did he send me down there?'

91

asked Bert, narrowing his eyes across the table. 'Want me to guess? He wanted someone down there to look around, to see if anythin' was going on down there. I'll bet you back that new hat you owe me that he told you to hunt mustangs down there for the same damned reason. I got no idea why, exactly, but the old cuss can't ride down there himself, but he wants to know if there is something goin' on down there —so he let you hunt horses, and he hired me an' sent me down to look around too.'

Snowy sat wiggling his toes and looking at them by the weak lantern-light, his leathery, square-jawed countenance more reflective than argumentative. Finally, he broke across Bert's thoughts with another of his dry remarks. 'Well, pardner, I'll tell you one thing—whatever we was supposed to see down there, we sure as hell saw it today, and we're in trouble up to our withers.

Now I got to get some sleep.'

Bert sat a while longer at the table before he, too, bedded down. In the morning he was still reflective, even when Snowy had their breakfast meat cooked and the coffee on the table, and they sat down opposite from one another to eat, so Snowy said, 'Did you swallow your tongue last night?'

Bert made a small smile. 'Did you ever have the feelin' there is somethin' you can almost reach, but not quite?'

Snowy washed down dry meat with hot coffee before answering. 'Yeah. In a saloon over in Tombstone one time there was a real pretty dancin' girl and...You don't want to hear about that.'

They went down to the barn to saddle up, although they had no destination in mind, and when they were passing inside where the perpetual gloom lingered, old Northfield hailed them from the house, and beckoned.

Snowy paused a long while before commenting. 'His friend upped and died last night. Now we got to dig a grave today. Well, hell, let's go get it over with.'

Snowy was wrong, Rattlesnake Rowe had not died, he was able to move his head and his hands, but he was still far too weak to do much else. But his mind was clear, and that was why Amos Northfield had summoned his rangemen to the house.

The three of them entered the bedroom and Rowe's eyes flickered past Northfield to the pair of younger men, darted back to Amos once, then the outlaw said, 'They followed me. There was four of 'em. By rights they should have found this place by now even though I dragged brush to cover my sign, and rode in creeks as much as I could. They're bound to show up.'

Snowy leaned in the doorway, coolly eyeing the wounded man. Bert and

Amos stepped farther into the room and old Amos pulled a chair around to sit down when Snowy said, 'Mister Rowe, I've never bucked the law in my life.'

Rattlesnake's eyes widened perceptibly. 'The law, hell. It's not the law.'

'Bounty hunters?' Bert enquired and got the same intent stare. 'No. I don't know who they are. They picked up my tracks outside Morgansville. I saw them a couple of times but they're damned good at stalking, even in open country.'

Snowy's scepticism had not diminished. 'If you only saw 'em a couple of times, and they were far back, how do you know it's not the law?'

'The law don't set up a bushwhack the way those bastards did,' stated the wounded outlaw. 'Two of 'em remained back. I tried to keep an eye peeled back there, and rode right down the gunbarrels of the other two. They must have ridden all night to get around me and get set.'

Snowy's broad low forehead got two deep furrows across it. 'That's more like bountymen.'

Rowe said, 'Like hell. They didn't try to kill me. Reward hunters would have done it on the spot.'

'Why wouldn't they want to kill you?' asked Snowy, gazing intently at Rattlesnake Rowe.

Rattlesnake lay there a moment as though gathering strength to go on, then he swung his glance over to Amos's face and did not look back for a long while, not until old Amos made a fluttery gesture with his hands and started to speak.

'Rattlesnake and me are friends. Been friends about five, six years.'

Snowy raised a hand to scratch the tip of his nose. His expression was rueful. Even Bert shifted stance and got a look of mild boredom on his face.

Amos saw the looks and perhaps was influenced by them, but he was clearly under considerable strain and was only speaking with very great reluctance. He was going to say it his way, whether he was repeating himself or not.

'He rode in back quite a few years on his way north up out of California. Rode for me all season. We got to be pretty good friends. Then he left, and only last winter on his way back down to California he came back. My place is about as isolated as a ranch can be. He was in trouble then too...Well, since he rode out the first time years back, and come back again last winter, a lot of things had happened around here.'

Amos Northfield looked at the faces opposite him, looked unhappily at Rattlesnake in his bed, then did not speak but instead reached into his pocket, withdrew something and flipped it over and Bert Osborne caught it. Snowy stepped ahead to look too. It was a piece of raw gold the size of a man's thumb-pad but a whole lot heavier.

Snowy looked up first. He stared steadily at old Northfield. 'Where'd you get it?'

Amos stared back. 'You know damned well where I got it.'

Snowy took the nugget and hefted it, examined it up close, then hefted it again as he faintly frowned in Northfield's direction. 'It wasn't a Mex myth, then, was it? I heard the story of that Spanish mine when I was a greenhorn just starting out. But that was a hundred miles south of here. I understood the mine was over there. I think the Messicans who told me the story believed that too.'

Northfield took his nugget and pocketed it as he began speaking again. 'That don't matter. The rest of the story is—I put gold in little sacks for a long while before Rattlesnake came back. I showed him the stuff. He said he'd take it to a town—Morgansville's closest—and sell it and fetch me back the money.

That's what he's been doin' for the past eight months.'

Bert blew out a big breath. 'And got shot for it.'

Rattlesnake smiled a little at Bert Osborne. 'That's why they didn't kill me. They'd never have found out where I was bringin' it from if I was dead, but if they got me out of the saddle…'

Snowy was staring at old Amos. After a long while he recovered partially and said, 'I'll be damned. How long have you known where the lost Spanish mine was?'

Northfield's craggy old rugged face closed down in a look of stubborn belligerence. 'I said, we wouldn't talk about the mine. Just about what Rattle-snake's worried about—those four bastards eventually working around all the ruses he used, and arrivin' out there in the yard.'

Bert looked from Snowy to the wounded outlaw. 'Why didn't you take it to different towns each time you cashed it in?'

Amos answered annoyedly. 'What other towns? Morgansville's the only town within a two-week ride from here. Anyway, if he'd spread it around, someone would still have maybe wondered; maybe a lot of folks would have wondered.'

Snowy broke up this discussion with a sour comment. 'Mister Northfield, we got three free-grazers mad as hornets, and now we got four gold-hunters willin' to kill to find your cache, or whatever it is you got. I'd like to live as long as you have, but right this minute my prospects for doin' it don't look very good.'

Northfield had evidently either already discussed this topic with Rattlesnake Rowe, or he had pondered it privately, but in either case he had an answer to put forth.

'Snowy, you're making thirty a

month and found with me right now. You and Bert...I'll up that to three hundred dollars a month.'

Bert eyed the old man without saying a word. Bank presidents didn't make that much. But Snowy was older and less susceptible to shock in something like this. He said, 'It's a pile of money, Amos, but at most we'd only draw it one month. After that we'd either be dead or they would, and most likely it'd be us. I'm no gunfighter. I don't think Bert is either. And there are the odds...' Snowy wagged his head. 'But I'll ride over to Morgansville if you want me to an' see if I can't find some fellers who'll take on that kind of an offer.'

Rattlesnake spoke for the first time in many minutes. He fixed Snowy Baker with a steady stare as he said, 'No, you won't do any such a damned thing. Even if you found some fellers, as soon as they figured out what the prize was— Amos's cache—they'd kill me in this bed and they'd kill Amos in his chair.'

Northfield arose and stood a moment until his bothersome knee-joints locked into place. 'Think on it,' he told Snowy, and led the way back out front to the veranda, where Bert, the last man to leave the house, gently closed the door. The old man did not press them, he simply looked them both in the eye, then nodded and went back inside.

They crossed to the bunkhouse, but heard a slight commotion down behind the barn and turned in the bunkhouse doorway to investigate.

It was Rattlesnake Rowe's breedy horse. He had a caulk-gash on his thigh. It was fresh enough to be still bleeding. They took the horse inside, cleansed the injury, which looked worse than it was, sprinkled powdered alum and powdered blue vitriol in the gash. The horse lunged ahead but Bert hauled him up short and talked to him. That vitriol stung like blue blazes.

Snowy put the powder pail back on a shelf and said, 'We better corral him by himself. In a stall, he's goin' to stand in one place and get stiff as a plank.'

Bert handed Snowy the shank. They walked out back, where Snowy walked out a short distance to turn the horse sharply on his injured side. The horse gimped, but from flesh-pain, not bone-pain, which was what Snowy had wanted to ascertain. It was not too difficult healing that kind of wound provided it did not go beyond the flesh to the bones and hip-socket. Bruised bone took a very long time to recover.

Bert was standing by the corral gate, holding it open as he watched Snowy lead the black horse toward him. Neither of them had any warning at all when the shot sounded from a fair distance out, and Snowy went down in a pile, the black horse snorted and pulled back, then stopped to look down at the man in front of him.

Bert was stunned for a matter of several seconds, then ran out, lifted Snowy in both arms and carried him into the barn. The black horse followed, because he did not know what else to do.

Snowy groaned when Bert put him down on the hardpan barn floor, raised an unsteady hand and felt the side of his head. There was blood there, but not very much. The bullet had ploughed a very thin streak no more than three inches long above Snowy's temple. An inch closer and it would have killed him. As it was, he sat up, fished for his bandanna, and held it to the wound as he looked around, then met Bert's anxious gaze.

Snowy said, 'Where was the son of a bitch?'

Bert unconsciously gestured. 'Out yonder, darn near the range of his carbine. Otherwise he'd have busted your head like a punky melon.'

'Did you see him?'

'Didn't look for him, carried you in here before he got off another round. How do you feel?'

'It don't hurt but I feel sort of weak. How bad is it?'

'Not too bad. Sort of a gouge is all, but it bled like you were a stuck hog.'

'Help me up,' Snowy said, and looked at the black horse, turned toward a stall door for support, then turned and looked at the black horse a second time, now with a little quizzical frown creasing his brow.

'Bert? You know what I think? I think if it'd been you leadin' that horse instead of me, he'd have tried to shoot you.'

Osborne, too, turned to stare at the patient-standing breedy black horse. 'He thought you were Rattlesnake?' asked Bert.

'That's my guess,' replied Snowy Baker. 'There's no reason for someone to want to shoot me. Not even those free-grazers got a good reason. It was you, not me that rode Dave down... Bert, if they shot me for Rattlesnake, then they don't know they hit Rattlesnake.'

Bert was thinking along different lines. He stood gazing out of the rear barn opening to the distant, empty terrain where that bushwhacker had been lying when he fired. As he faced the older man again he put his thoughts into words.

'I'll tell you something, Snowy. We're stuck here. Just saddle a horse and ride out there, and see. Whether it's the free-grazers or the fellers who shot Rattlesnake, they're out there, and, sure as hell, they're watching the place. We're stuck here, unless we can slip away after dark.'

Snowy lowered the bloody bandanna, studied it for a while, then raised it to his injury again as he said, 'Give me a hand to the bunkhouse...If you want to slip away, go right ahead, but me—I'm goin' to find the son of a bitch who shot me.'

CHAPTER 7

TOWARD EVENING

Old Amos glowered at the small bandage on Snowy Baker's head and stamped to the bunkhouse table to sit at one of the benches. 'I told you boys a couple of days ago—stay in the open.'

Snowy snorted. 'But you didn't tell us *why,* and that could get a man killed.'

Bert was cleaning up the mess they had made cleansing the injury and bandaging it. He came up with something both his companions thought about. He said, 'It likely wasn't the fellers who were after Rattlesnake. Whoever shot Snowy was aiming for his head, and that would have been a killin' shot if it'd held a little more to the right. The men who shot Rattlesnake didn't aim to kill him when they ambushed him, so why would they try to do it now? I'll put my money on the free-grazers.'

It was a theory and nothing more, but it helped pass the time and it gave them something to think about. Amos left the bunkhouse, and Snowy went with him, ostensibly to relate what had occurred to Rattlesnake Rowe, but actually Snowy needed a good big jolt of whiskey.

Bert returned to the barn, with the tie-down hanging loose at his holster, and stood a long time in shadows, looking out where that bushwhacker had been hiding.

There was nothing out there, nor did he expect to see anything. He moved across to a position where he could see the distant grazing horses. They were drowsily standing in pleasant warmth, full and contented. Not a one of them was showing curiosity. If there had been an alien scent, or any kind of movement, the loose-stock would be interested.

Bert saddled a horse from the southerly working corrals, but he did it inside the barn, then he went to the bunkhouse for his booted carbine and strapped that to the saddle, also inside the barn. He even mounted in there, something no horseman and very few cowboys ever did. Finally, he rode directly westward to find the place where the bushwhacker had been lying.

He found it.

There was a shallow arroyo with a scooped out place at its northernmost extremity. The man had left his horse there, had crept down the arroyo until it became only a slight depression directly west of the barn, and that was where he had fired from. There was no shell casing, but there were plenty of clear boot-tracks. He squatted out there, studying the tracks, moved up them almost to the place where the horse had stood hobbled, then he swung up and traced out the route the ambusher had used in departing, and although the man had ridden northward at a long lope, eventually he had altered course toward the west, and about the time Bert was ready to give up and head for the home-place, the rider changed course again and went straight southward in the direction of the blue sage country.

When Bert got back to the barn and was unsaddling, Snowy came along looking little the worse for his brush with death, and asked what Bert had found out yonder.

'Tracks of a shod horse makin' a big sashay up and around, then headin' south,' Bert replied. 'No shell casing, nothing else that amounted to much. How do you feel?'

Snowy smiled. 'Mean.'

Bert laughed as he flung his outfit over the saddle-pole and took the horse out back to the corral. When he returned, Snowy was waiting. 'You want to ride down yonder after dark tonight?' he asked very casually, his gaze fixed upon the younger man.

Bert went to lean on the pole before answering. 'What for?'

'Every time we've tried it in daylight they've seen us first. I was thinking, maybe if we could catch one of those bastards...'

'What did Mister Northfield say about this?'

'I didn't talk about it to him.'

Bert gazed at Snowy Baker, then straightened up off the pole. 'All right. I guess we might as well.'

'Otherwise,' opinioned Snowy Baker, 'they're goin' to nail us one at a time, while we're mindin' our own business. Thing is, Bert, we're sittin' around the ranch. A man never gets in his licks while he's standin' around, does he?'

They went to the bunkhouse to eat and play blackjack until dusk, then went down to rig out their horses, and this time Snowy also carried a saddlegun slung in its scabbard under his *rosadero*.

They had not gone near the mainhouse, which bothered Bert a little but which did not bother Snowy at all as they rode southward for several miles. Then angled south-easterly because, as Snowy said, those free-grazers had a camp somewhere which would be visible from a landswell, especially if they were cooking supper.

'Mister Northfield won't approve, most likely,' murmured Bert, as they were angling toward the same landswell where they had first sighted the livestock.

They did not reach the landswell before they saw a distant, low glow in the settling night. Snowy reined to a halt and studied the cooking-fire for a while, then looked at his companion. 'Did you ever stalk anyone before?' he asked, and Bert shook his head. 'Never had any reason to—and if you ask me, that fire's too damned far east. The cattle been driftin' west for several days. Why would the free-grazers have a camp five or six miles behind their cattle?'

Snowy did not answer, he turned back to studying the distant glow, then stood in his stirrups to look elsewhere, but there was no other firelight anywhere in sight, so he sat down again. He said, 'Let's go,' and turned his horse eastward, holding it to a steady course among the uneven foothill, rolling country parallel to the firelight but more than a mile north of it. When they could see the source of the fire, which appeared to be a camp out in the crumbly-earth territory of the blue sage plain, Snowy leaned to dismount as he spoke.

'You stay here with the horses. Most

of all, we don't want to be set afoot. I'll go down and look. If I can get one I'll do it, if not I won't risk my neck trying.'

Bert dismounted, accepted Snowy's reins and watched his partner strike out without taking along his carbine. Perhaps Snowy thought any trouble which might erupt would be at handgun range, and if he thought that he was probably right. In the darkness a man could get much closer than he could in daylight.

Bert made a smoke behind his horse, lighted it inside his hat, and straightened up to listen and look. The night was silent; if the cattle had been this far eastward it would not have been silent.

A rodent-hunting owl soared past very low without making a sound and only occasionally pumping its wings, so intent upon finding a meal he did not notice the pair of horses or the motionless man standing with them.

Miles southward, down across the

open country, some little Swift foxes yapped, making a sound halfway between that of coyotes and squealing rabbits, and almost simultaneously several coyotes on the move to the west sounded. Bert listened to the coyotes to ascertain in which direction they were foraging; it seemed to be eastward.

He finished his smoke and curbed rising impatience. The cooking-fire was still cheerily burning; there had been no indication by either movement across the lighted area, or sounds, that anything unusual had happened down there.

Fifteen minutes later, Snowy came walking up out of the darkness. He said, 'It's not the free-grazers.'

Bert cocked an eyebrow. 'Maybe Rattlesnake's friends from Morgansville?'

Snowy lifted his hat to scratch vigorously before replying. 'Maybe. I crawled as close as I dared to hear their talk, but they were playin' cards on a blanket and didn't say much of anything. But it's four fellers, and that's the number Rattlesnake gave.'

Snowy took his reins and swung across leather. Bert also mounted, and as Snowy struck out due westerly Bert assumed he had something on his mind.

'Find the free-graze camp,' Snowy explained and kept on riding.

They did not leave the foothills, not even after they detected a fresh scent of cattle. What Snowy did not want to do was to encounter livestock, especially in their beds in the darkness. Nothing would spook half-wild cattle quicker than a pair of riders suddenly appearing among them. Frightened cattle would run and, whether they started a general stampede or not, their agitation would let the men who were also out there somewhere know there was something moving through the night which might be enemies.

They did not locate the camp. Bert was puzzled about that. The free-grazers had to have one, and even if they had already eaten there should still be some firelight showing in the night.

He was pondering this when his partner suddenly hauled back to an abrupt halt, sitting erect in the saddle, peering southward. Bert did not see the rider until he moved, making a slow pass well above bedded cattle. He halted again below the landswell which shielded Northfield's riders, tipped his head to match-flare and lit a smoke.

Dave!

Snowy shot Bert a look and a bleak smile, but said nothing until the bull-necked, tow-headed rangeman eased out his horse and continued his nighthawk-riding. 'All we got to do is catch the son of a bitch,' said Snowy. 'And not get shot doin' it, or rouse the damned countryside.' He did not mean just the other free-grazers, he also meant those half-wild, wicked-horned cattle; in darkness they would charge in all directions. There were a lot of stories about men who had died under stampeding cattle in darkness.

This time Bert swung off and held up his reins. He did not say a word as Snowy took the reins and offered a bit of advice. 'Get him from behind or let him go. Don't start a big battle.'

Bert hooked both spurs around the horn of his saddle and did as Snowy had done back six or eight miles, he left the carbine in its boot as he started foward, keeping to the cover of the landswell as much as he could.

Nighthawking was a monotonous chore at best and because it was ordinarily done by men who had already put in a long day, unless the weather was threatening or there was imminent danger of predators, riders dozed in the saddle as their horses carried them in a huge circle around the bedded cattle.

Even so, an unmounted man attacking a mounted man faced unique problems, unless fate intervened as it did for Bert Osborne when he was just about to abandon his stalk of the tow-headed man on his shuffling horse, and Dave reined to a halt, swung down and thumbed back his hat as he stood with his face towards the cattle to pee.

Bert came up very carefully, watching the horse as much as the man, and true to his suspicion, the horse detected him when the man did not, and the horse tried to twist for a better look although Dave had both reins firmly in a one-handed grip as he growled at the horse, and yanked on the reins to stop his mount from fidgeting.

Dave was fully occupied when Bert got within five yards of him, with the horse between them, then moving around into plain sight, palmed his Colt, and cocked it.

Dave froze at the sound of a gun

being cocked behind him. For five seconds there was not a sound. Bert said, 'Shuck your gun.'

Dave obeyed, and recognised the voice. 'What do you want?' he asked.

Bert ignored that. 'Face me, turn around.'

Dave turned slowly, eyed Bert, then looked elsewhere as though he expected Snowy to also be there. When their eyes met and held Bert gave his orders. 'Lift your boots one at a time, I want a good look at the soles.'

Dave obeyed, beginning to scowl a little. When he had showed both soles he said, 'What the hell are you doing?'

Bert did not reply to that question either. 'Where are Moran and Kendall?'

Dave still leaned on the horse as he replied. 'In camp, about a couple of miles westerly. In a draw with some trees in it.' He cast another foraging glance around for Snowy, for the outline of anyone at all who might be with

Bert Osborne.

Bert gestured for Dave to move away from the horse, walked over to retrieve the gun Dave had tossed down, then gestured again as he said, 'Walk east, lead the horse and stay ahead of me on the left side of the horse. Just walk, understand?'

Dave did not say whether he understood or not. He turned and started walking, trudging along with his head down a little, finally recovered from his surprise, and angry now, all the way through.

When they reached Snowy the tow-headed rangeman said, 'You think catchin' me is goin' to help you any? Well, it damned well ain't!'

Snowy leaned on his saddlehorn, staring at the younger man. 'You bush-whackin' bastard,' he said softly.

Before Dave could speak, Bert said, 'It wasn't him, Snowy. The boot-soles are different from the tracks I found out there.'

Dave turned perplexedly from one of them to the other. 'Bushwhacking? What in hell are you talkin' about? If we wanted your hides, we wouldn't sneak around to get 'em. For your kind we wouldn't have to do—'

Snowy snarled at Dave. 'Shut up and stay shut up!' He scowled at Bert. 'You didn't tell me you found boot-tracks out there.'

'I told you I found sign,' stated Bert, 'and I'm not goin' to stand out here arguing. What do you want to do with this one?'

Snowy checked something he had been about to say and looked at Dave again, but did not speak for a long while, not until he had settled something in his mind, then he turned toward Bert again. 'Let this one lead us to the camp of the other two—are you sure you'd know the boot-marks?'

Bert answered while leathering his

Colt and pulling his horse to him. 'Yeah, I'd know them.' When he settled into the saddle he growled at Dave. 'Get astride, and *walk* that darned horse. Head for your camp and keep your mouth closed!' He was still annoyed with his partner.

CHAPTER 8

SOMETHING TO THINK ABOUT

The reason they had not seen the free-grazers' campfire became obvious after they had been riding westward for about an hour, and Dave angled away from the vast sagebrush plain; it was not out in the open country the way that other campfire had been, it was in a stretch of foothill country where several arroyos converged to create a rather large, wide depression in the land which had a fine stand of grass in it as well as several large trees.

When Dave halted to look at his captors, scowling resentfully, Bert handed him his sixgun from which the loads had been extracted. 'Ride on in,' he said. Snowy nodded agreement and the trio went down a grassy gradual slope where for the first time they saw dying coals and the customary litter of a horse-camp. There was no wagon, which Snowy noted because he had never given up the idea that there should be one.

Two lumpy shapes near the dying fire turned out to be men in bedrolls. There were several hobbled horses out a short distance where several lengths of rope had been stretched among the trees to prevent the animals from going in a northerly search for grass.

Dave sat his saddle while Snowy and Bert swung down, stepped over and wakened Moran and Kendall by simply placing cold gunbarrels against their faces. Dave looked more disgusted now than belligerent, as the pair of older men sat up in their blankets. They had coiled shellbelts and holstered sixguns within inches of their blankets, but now they had no chance to reach to arm themselves and after they had been awakened and were sitting up, Bert and Snowy kicked the coiled belts farther away.

Wood Kendall said nothing. He looked at the armed men, looked past where Dave was sitting, his holster showing the saw-handle of a sixgun, and only moved when Wesley Moran spoke to Bert Osborne, whose cocked Colt was a foot from his face.

'You couldn't do it by daylight, so you had to sneak around in the dark like Messicans.'

Bert turned, picked up Moran's boots, up-ended them near the feebly glowing fire-ring and studied them for a moment before tossing them aside and walking over to do the same with Kendall's boots. Both the sitting men watched this without a word, but Dave explained from the saddle. 'They think one of us tried to bushwhack the feller with the white hair. They're lookin' for imprints.'

Snowy turned and snarled. 'I told you to shut up and keep shut up!' He then turned to face Bert. The younger man shook his head. 'Not unless one of 'em owns two pairs of boots,' he said.

Snowy leathered his gun and went over to paw through the saddlery and camp equipment. Kendall spoke for the first time in that quiet, calm voice of his. 'None of us got two pair of boots, mister. In this business you're lucky if you own one pair.' Kendall then started to roll out of his blankets, and Bert watched him but did not stop him.

Moran, too, rolled out to go after his boots and tug them on. He was still sitting down when he said, 'If we wanted your hides we wouldn't sneak up on you to get 'em.'

Dave finally swung to the ground. He methodically began removing the saddle, blanket and bridle from his horse. He hunkered down to buckle the hobbles into place, then arose and gave the horse a light pat to start it hopping out where the other horses were.

Snowy returned from pawing through the effects and stood by the fire faintly frowning. Bert picked up the weapons of the free-grazers and waited for Snowy to make up his mind about what they would do now. Snowy blew out a big breath and looked over where Wesley Moran was standing up to tuck in his shirt-tails.

'Get your cattle moving tomorrow and keep them moving,' he said.

Moran looked at Baker as he finished with his shirt. He seemed more unwilling to answer back than when they had met before.

Wood Kendall was dropping an old hat upon the back of his head as he finally said, 'You had to bring in help, didn't you?' He made a careless eastward gesture. 'We watched 'em this afternoon. They scouted around, then rode off in the direction you fellers always head for—north-westerly. That's where the home-place is, isn't it?'

Bert was watching Snowy to see if he had figured this out. Evidently he had, because without changing expression he replied to the free-grazer. 'It's easier to hire help than you'd think.'

'That kind of help,' stated Kendall, 'is always easy to hire.'

'Are you goin' to pull out in the morning or not?' Snowy asked.

Moran broke in to say, 'We're goin' to hunt up the home-place and talk to the feller you boys work for. That's what we're goin' to do, an' if we can't work somethin' out with him, then we'll maybe move along...There's still an awful lot of feed out here.' Moran paused, then also said, 'Buyin' graze goes against the grain, but maybe we can work somethin' out. Not with cash, but maybe we can work somethin' out.'

To Bert, the change in the belligerent free-grazers seemed to arise from their belief that those four men camping about eight miles eastward had been hired to help Bert and Snowy fight for the Northfield grazing territory. For the first time since Bert had been around these men they were not threatening.

Snowy was silent a long while. So long in fact that Dave went over to squat near the fire and feed sticks into the coals until he had a flame showing, then to place a battered, filthy coffeepot upon two stones where the fire would reach.

Snowy approached Bert and leaned to quietly say, 'Let's get back.' Bert was perfectly agreeable, so they went to their horses, swung up, and with three baleful sets of eyes watching, rode back up out of the arroyo on their way home.

Snowy was quiet for almost two miles, then he laughed and looked at his companion. 'There's some kind of fate that looks out for old men and damned fools...You could have bowled me over with a feather when it came out they thought those other fellers work for Mex Hat too.'

'As long as they don't ride down there and talk to those other fellers,' said Bert. Then he, too, smiled.

They loped for a half-hour, walked for as long again, then loped again and by the time they reached the yard there was a chill in the air to indicate dawn was coming.

It was still dark when they cared for their mounts and trooped to the bunk-house, but by the time they had the stove fired up for breakfast, the sky was gunmetal grey and brightening steadily toward a pale shade of pewter-blue.

Snowy shaved first at the wash-rack out back. Bert was out there afterwards when Amos Northfield came striding down from the main-house. They offered him coffee, which he took at the table, then, as Snowy began explaining where they had been last night and what they had done, Amos forgot the coffee and showed that darkly menacing scowl he seemed to use about half the time.

'If you were goin' to do something like that,' he growled at them, 'why didn't you go after those other four. Sure as hell they're after Rattlesnake.'

Snowy answered testily. 'I just told you—I couldn't catch one of them away from the others, and I wasn't goin' to get myself shot doin' something rash.'

Old Amos's head came up. 'Rash! What the hell do you think you did last night? Where were those free-grazers camped?'

'In a sort of wide swale near the foothills about four, five miles west of the—'

'Did it have trees growing in it, and a little creek?'

Neither Bert nor Snowy had seen a creek, but they affirmed the location of the trees. Amos stared at the ajar door for a long while, then said, 'I want 'em out of there. I don't give a damn what they offer for the grazin' right, I want 'em clean out of that area. In fact I want 'em plumb off my land.'

Bert filled a cup at the stove and went over to sit down at the table. 'Then just tell 'em to move along when they show up in the yard today.' He grinned at Snowy past the old man's shoulder. 'Tell 'em they got until tomorrow to be on the move or you'll send us, and those fellers down there to stampede their cattle out of the country.'

Amos abruptly rose and stalked out of the bunkhouse, head down as he turned in the direction of the main-house, and Snowy waited a discreet few moments to say, 'He's not crazy, Eh? Yesterday they could graze, today they can't. What the hell do you call that sort of thinking?'

Bert sipped coffee, did not comment,

and sat in thought for a long while. Snowy went over to fry their breakfast, looking pensive. When he brought over the two plates he had an idea to put before Bert Osborne.

'I think that damned mine is close by where those fellers got their cattle.'

Bert fished for his clasp-knife to spear fried meat with before commenting. 'Then he's *not* crazy, is he?'

Snowy was not willing to go that far, but he said, 'It's somewhere around on that damned prairie, sure as I'm a foot tall.'

Bert ate methodically. He was not interested in the old Spanish mine. 'How long's it been out there?'

'Hell, I don't know. Couple hundred years, I guess. Why?'

'Because if folks have been searching for it for two hundred years without any success, and if the old man isn't goin' to tell you where it is—you're goin' to be wanderin' around out there until you die and never find it. That's why.'

Snowy began to wolf down the food. He had no more to say about the gold-mine. Perhaps he would have, by the time they were finishing their meal, but a man's distant shout roused him. He went to the door and stood there for half a minute before speaking to Bert over his shoulder.

'Here come the free-grazers. They sure didn't waste much time trackin' us.'

The loose-horses, which were about a mile north-westward, saw strangers crossing the south slope of Northfield's big meadow, and began to circle and run, heads and tails up. They would not come that far off their natural feeding ground to investigate, but the appearance of strangers gave them a wonderful excuse to rush back and forth, snort and then race away and halt to turn and snort again.

Snowy went to the main-house to alert

Amos Northfield to the nearness of the free-grazers, and Bert leaned in the bunkhouse doorway, watching the distant riders. Evidently the free-grazers doubted the welcome they might expect, because when one of them had called out, all three of them had been just crossing over the far lip of the most southerly extremity of the big meadow.

Their slow, prudent approach and the fact that they had sung out inclined Bert to believe they had come directly to the Northfield home-place, and had not gone eastward to talk with those four strangers camped over there. He let go a little sigh of relief over that because it was one thing which had worried him all morning.

If they could settle with the free-grazers, and the other men, separately, they had a ghost of a chance. If the strangers and free-grazers worked out an accord between them, that would make bad odds for the two able men at

the Northfield ranch, the one old man,
and the bedridden outlaw.

CHAPTER 9

STALKERS

Moran, Wood Kendall and tow-headed Dave halted in front of the bunkhouse without alighting. Bert leaned in the doorway, stoically exchanging looks with them until Moran asked where the owner was, then Bert jerked his head. 'At the main-house.'

Moran eyed the residence as he also said, 'Did you fellers tell him we were coming?'

'We told him,' Bert replied.

Kendal looked around. 'Where are the other fellers?'

Bert shrugged. 'What difference does

that make; you want to talk to Mister Northfield.'

The door slammed over at the main-house. Snowy and old Amos stood briefly on the porch, looking to where the free-grazers were sitting their saddles. The old man had a sixgun belted low around his middle and was wearing a relatively new grey hat. He struck out toward the bunkhouse with that bear-like thrusting stride, and Bert, watching the free-grazers, thought they were impressed by the old man's hulking size and his craggy face.

Snowy pointed and said, 'That's their head In'ian, Mister Northfield.'

The old man fixed a cold look upon Wesley Moran. Bert was sure Snowy had primed the old man because when he spoke old Amos was gruff. 'What d'you want?'

Moran eyed Northfield calmly. 'Came to talk about usin' your feed down yonder.'

'You been usin' it,' exclaimed the old man, not once taking his eyes off Wes Moran. 'You been trespassin' on it ever since you came into the sagebrush prairie.'

'You own all that land down there, Mister Northfield?'

'Seven thousand acres of it. Deeded land, mister, ever' damned acre of it.'

Moran shifted slightly in the saddle. It was customary to invite riders to dismount in a man's yard. Moran gazed over at the main-house and Bert suspected he was probably thinking there were armed men over there watching for the first sign of trouble.

Then Moran said, 'We'd like to work somethin' out so's we can keep the cattle down there for another week or two. If you don't aim to use the feed...an' we got some tender-footed critters...'

The old man surprised Bert. When he had been in the bunkhouse only an hour or so earlier, he had been adamant about wanting the free-grazers off his land. Now, he scowled at Moran and said, 'Work out what? What you got in mind?'

Moran relaxed slightly. 'Well, Mister Northfield, we got no ready money. Won't have until we sell off, and that don't seem likely until we get out of this country to some place where they got corrals and shipping chutes near a town.'

'Go on. Spit it out, I don't have all day to stand out here.'

Moran gazed steadily at Amos Northfield. 'We'll give you ten head of cattle for your grass for three weeks.'

The old man did not even hesitate. 'Twenty head—cows with calves—I make the selection—and you can stay a month.'

Wood Kendall showed a small, appreciative grin. Dave just sat there looking and listening. Bert almost smiled too. The old man might be past the age to ride and shoot, or even to see very well, but there was nothing at all wrong with his bartering instincts.

Wes Moran hesitated, still gazing downward. Eventually he pulled off a roping glove and leaned to extend a hand. 'Trade,' he said, and old Amos strode over, gripped the hand, pumped it once, and the transaction was completed.

Then the old man surprised Bert a second time. 'Just two things,' he told Wes Moran. 'Move your camp out of that arroyo, and keep a close watch on those four cattle-thieves camped six or eight miles east of you.'

Moran stared. 'We figured those were your men.'

'Not on your damned life,' growled old Amos. 'They been scoutin' up my cattle on the north range, and sure as hell they've scouted up your herd too.'

Dave spoke up. 'Wes, we seen 'em scoutin' around.'

Moran ignored that. He turned a bland gaze upon Bert, still slouching in the bunkhouse doorway, then looked over to where Snowy was standing, and Snowy, probably feeling slightly self-conscious about having helped to foster that idea last night that those four strangers were indeed Mexican Hat riders, simply shrugged.

Wood Kendall spoke for the first time. He quietly said, 'You have much trouble with cattle-thieves in this territory, Mister Northfield?'

Amos answered gruffly. 'Mister, I used to run eleven hundred head. Now, I'm down to just a hundred or so pairs and some big steers. A lot I sold off, and a lot just weren't out there when I'd round up.' Amos fixed Kendall with a hard look. 'You're one hell of a distance from a town, and even then the law over at Morgansville's about as worthless as teats on a man. This blue sage country is made to order for horse-thieves and rustlers. I always been my own law—but that hasn't helped a hell of a lot.'

Wesley Moran was slowly putting on his glove as he listened to Amos. Then he turned and cast an impassive glance at Kendall and Dave before lifting his reinhand and facing Amos again.

'Suppose,' he said, 'your riders helped us for a day or two. We let the cattle get scattered to hell. We just figured those men had been hired by you to back up these two fellers. If you got rustlers on your range, we got to get the cattle in a couple of miles closer.'

Amos pondered that, then turned toward Snowy, who said nothing, so he looked over toward the bunkhouse doorway and Bert shrugged as though to indicate it was Amos's decision. Northfield scowled at Moran as he said, 'For a few days is all—and if there's any trouble between you fellers and my riders...'

Wood Kendall made that faint, tough

little grin again and said, 'There won't be any trouble, Mister Northfield. Every time we've had any with those two fellers, somehow or another we come off second best.'

Bert almost smiled too, but no one else did. Moran glanced past old Amos to Snowy. 'In the morning?'

Snowy nodded, and the free-grazers turned to ride out of the yard. As they did this, Bert caught a very brief, very distant flash of bright sunlight off metal. It had been up the meadow eastward and near that distant landswell where he had seen what had happened to be a horseman once before, but this time he could not make out movement, although he was confident there had been some.

He said nothing about this as Amos turned to go back to the main-house, then halted a few yards away, turned and spoke. 'Snowy, you reckon they believed that?'

146

Snowy thought so. 'Yeah. But how long they'll believe it is something different.'

The old man thought a moment before speaking again. 'If you boys stirred them up a little against the rustlers and all...'

Snowy smiled. 'We'll see,' he replied, and walked over to the bunkhouse porch while Amos Northfield strode back to the main-house. When he stepped into overhang shade, though, he was faintly frowning. 'It seemed like a good idea when the old man told them those were cattle-thieves, but right now I don't know.'

Bert did not know either, but for some perverse reason the idea appealed to him. 'It might work,' he told the other man. 'If it don't work, Snowy, we're not goin' to be a hell of a lot worse off than we were.'

Snowy walked inside and dropped down at the old table, still troubled.

147

'One other thing, Bert. When we go down yonder to help bring the cattle in closer, old Amos'll be alone with his friend.'

Bert, remembering the distant flash, filled two cups with coffee as he considered this fresh aspect of their dilemma. As he placed a cup before Snowy Baker and sat opposite him, he said, 'Maybe, if those free-grazers are stirred up enough, we could talk them into going rustler-hunting first, and cattle-gatherin' second.'

Snowy picked up his cup. 'Yeah, maybe. Old Amos knows those two-legged carrion-eaters are out there, so he'll keep watch from the main-house.' Snowy drank and put the cup down. 'Anyway, that's up to him.' Snowy fished for his tobacco and papers and gazed over at Bert. 'All I wanted was to maybe catch a few wild horses. All you wanted was a ridin' job for the season, and you know what?'

'What?'

Snowy was troughing the paper when he said, 'We could get killed, that's what.'

They saddled two horses about noon and rode southward until they could overlook the sagebrush prairie. Cattle down there looked no larger than big ants, and for a fact the free-grazers had indeed allowed them to scatter far and wide. Snowy said it was a wonder only three men had ever been able to hold that many cattle together, then he also opinioned that Moran, Kendall and Dave had to be tophands or they never would have got this far with their herd.

Snowy left it up to Bert where they went from the rim of the sagebrush prairie, and Bert, with curiosity prompting him to do it, dropped to the lower side of the foothill rolling country and reined off eastward. Snowy thought he was looking for that bushwhacker-camp they had seen last night, but what

Bert wanted to find was fresh tracks in the direction of that brilliant flash he had seen hours earlier.

They were miles east of the free-graze camp when the faint echo of a gunshot sounded. Bert whirled and stood in his stirrups but saw nothing. 'Too far off,' exclaimed Snowy. 'It could have been one of Moran's fellers shootin' a varmint, wolf maybe.'

There was no second gunshot. Bert struck out again, found a gravelly roll of land with a few stunted trees atop it and rode up there. From that point of vantage they could look down to where the campfire had been the night before. There was no one down there, not even any horses.

Bert turned northward down the far side of the gravelly hill and kept pointing north until they were at the far upper end of Northfield's meadow, which was all open country. What trees existed were a considerable distance ahead, and scattered along the upper side of the big meadow.

Bert zigzagged until he found what he sought. Fresh shod-horse tracks. Where they halted to look, he told Snowy what he had seen about the time Moran and his riders were leaving the yard and Snowy shook his head. 'You're the damndest feller I ever knew for keepin' things to himself. Last night you never said anythin' about boot-tracks. Today...' He continued to wag his head in disapproval.

They backtracked for two miles and found where the horseman had come up into the meadow from farther southward, riding in a big half-circle as though he had not wanted to be in sight of anyone at the home-place.

'Like a wolf,' Snowy said. 'Bert, I got a feelin' we're buckin' some darned *coyote* manhunters.'

They turned northward for an hour, saw more fresh tracks up there, then, since they were in the general vicinity, rode west until they found the same Mexican Hat cattle they had ridden through before, and over there they lost the shod-horse sign; grazing cattle had effectively scrubbed them out with their own tracks.

The sun was high, it was getting downright hot, there was very little shade, and the horses were thirsty, so they scouted up the only watercourse which held cattle in this kind of country, got into some willow-shade over there, dismounted, slipped the bridles, loosened their cinchas, and had a smoke in cool shade while the horses drank, then picked creekside grass for a while.

Snowy stretched out, placed his hat over his face and said, 'At least the free-grazers stay out in the open. Those other sons of bitches give me the creeps; they're like In'ians the way they skulk around. Like a pack of wolves, always spyin' and keepin' out of sight.' He killed his smoke, lifted his hat and looked up to where Bert was standing. 'You want to know why the old man told Moran to move his camp?'

Bert knew what was coming and dropped his smoke to stamp it out before saying, 'Yeah. Because you think that old mine is around there.'

'That's exactly what I think. And what's more—'

Bert interrupted as he squatted and tipped down his hat against sunglare. 'You want to know what *I* think? I think if you'll sit up and pretend like you're earnin' that three hundred dollars a month, I'll show you something.'

Snowy lifted his hat, groaned as he arose into a sitting posture, then pushed the old hat lower over his forehead as Bert pointed with his left arm and did not speak.

There was a horseman sitting in plain sight in the middle distance. He had not seen the pair of rangemen in willow-shade beside the creek, and unless they moved among all that mottled shade, he was not going to see them.

The man was closer than he probably had intended to get to anyone who might see him. They could make out that he was astride a seal-brown horse, that he was carrying a saddlegun under his fender, and was smoking a cigarette as he studied the fat cattle southward. He did not seem to be troubled, and he certainly did not act as though he had any inkling there were two men almost within Winchester range of him.

Snowy watched the stranger for a long while before speaking. 'It's none of the free-grazers, Bert. You know what I think? Hell, maybe old Amos hit the nail on the head by accident when he made out like those bastards were cattle-thieves.'

Bert said nothing. He sat motionlessly in speckled shade, watching the stranger and thinking. Eventually he said, 'We'd never catch him. The minute we came out of the shade he'd see us. But just for the hell of it, let's get across the creek and if he has to water his horse or get a drink...'

It was relatively easy to take the horses through the yellow thicket and get upon the opposite shore of the creek without attracting attention. The deeper they got into the willows the more they were hidden, and when they reached the far side after splashing through water as clear as glass—and sending trout-minnows scattering wildly in all directions—unless the stranger rode directly to the creek where they were waiting and watching, and found their fresh tracks, he would not see them at all.

He sat out there for a long while, killed his smoke, then eased ahead to walk his seal-brown horse down closer to the cattle. He was no novice; he knew exactly how close to get before the cattle spooked. He halted again, for a closer inspection of the critters, then turned as Snowy and Bert had done, paralleling the warily watchful cattle on his way toward the creek.

Bert bridled his horse, looped the reins to a willow tree and without saying a word sat down to shed his spurs, then arose and started walking carefully southward where the stranger would eventually reach the creek. He did not even glance back to see if Snowy was following, but the older man was back there, pulling loose the tie-down thong over his holstered Colt as he moved southward.

Once, Snowy caught up and softly said, 'Watch him like a damned hawk. He's got us outgunned with that carbine.'

Bert pressed close to the willows, not only for the protective shade they provided, but also because they masked his moving form. He had never stalked a man before. Snowy had, but there was really nothing much to be learned which did not come by instinct.

They could only catch intermittent glimpses as the rider came closer, could not really see him very well at all, except as a moving outline, until they were southward, in the vicinity of where he halted to dismount, then, motionless in a fly-infested thicket, they saw his face for the first time as he led the horse up to drink and shoved back his hat.

He was a man of about average height, lean and lithe with a darkly tanned face. His features were slightly hawkish, his mouth was a slit and his jaw was square and blunt. He had lived in the same trousers and shirt for some time, judging from their appearance; they were faded and stained. The only distinctive thing Bert and Snowy could see was the way the man wore his black-stocked sixgun; low, in a flash-out holster with the upper protective leather near the hammer significantly cut away. The holster was not tied to his leg, but it fitted close and hung perfectly.

If he was a rangerider, then he had to be an unusual one, for while he looked the part, he did not wear his gun like any cowboy Bert Osborne had ever seen.

His seal-brown horse was a young, strong, sleek animal, built for both speed and endurance, and the man's outfit was pure Southwestern from the rawhide reins and romal to the silver horn-cap.

Bert leaned, lifted out his weapon very carefully, and when the horse was finished drinking and the man stepped ahead as he shoved back his hat to kneel and also drink, Bert took two big onward steps, raised his Colt, reached with his free hand to part the willows, and as the man knelt with both hands pressed palms down against the soft earth, Bert spoke.

'Not a move!'

The stranger's shoulders stiffened, his head came up in total surprise. He had very dark eyes which looked steadily at the gunbarrel fifteen feet in front of him, then very slowly went higher, to the face of the man holding that gun. He did not move anything but his eyes. He saw Snowy too, but the astonishment had been complete, the man hung there for five seconds as motionless as a stone.

Snowy splashed back across the creek, went around behind the stranger and lifted his gun away, then cocked it and pointed it as he said, 'Stand up! Now walk out of the willows!'

The stranger obeyed each time something was said to him. When Bert crossed the creek, gun hanging at his side, the stranger finally found his voice.

In a placating tone he said, 'All right ...Now what?'

Snowy gestured. 'Both hands in front. Who are you and what are you doing out here?'

The black-eyed man relaxed slightly. 'Be damned careful,' he said to Snowy. 'That gun's got a hair-trigger.'

Snowy did not ease up his finger which was curled inside the trigger-guard. 'Who are you?' he asked again.

'Name is Bart Horn. I'm passin' through on my way to Morgansville.'

Bert said, 'Sit down, Mister Horn, and shove your feet straight out.'

Horn obeyed again, black eyes fixed upon Bert, who leaned and remained in that position for a long while before straightening up, then returned the stranger's hard gaze. 'Just passin' through, Mister Horn?'

The seated man nodded but did not speak.

Bert shook his head slightly. 'Like hell, *amigo*...Snowy, here's your bushwacker.'

'You plumb sure?'

Bert smiled bleakly at the stranger. 'Plumb sure.'

Snowy's finger perceptibly tightened

on the hair-trigger and the seated man spoke quickly. 'Don't squeeze! Listen; I never saw either of you boys before, so help me. I just came down through a pass back yonder in the mountains and saw these cattle and stopped to look at them, and—'

Snowy said, 'You lyin' bastard. Stand up; I never shot a man sittin' down in my life. *Stand up!*'

Horn arose, but slightly crouched. Snowy took one rearward step to widen the distance between them, the cocked, hair-triggered sixgun less than fifteen feet from its owner.

Bert held his breath; he did not know whether Snowy would kill the bushwhacker or not, but if he did regardless of any justification he might feel right now, the man was still unarmed, and that would be murder.

Snowy's face was impassive. He let Horn lean over there, scarcely breathing for ten seconds, then Snowy spoke again.

'Where are your friends, those other three sons of bitches?'

It was no time to pretend ignorance. Lying when a man's life was hanging by a thread would only put him closer to oblivion.

'Down south behind the ranchyard.'

'Stalkin' the place?' exclaimed Snowy.

'Watching it,' said the bushwhacker.

'To get a clean shot?' Bert asked, and although Bart Horn did not take his eyes off Snowy and the cocked sixgun, he said, 'Lookin' for someone is all. We're lookin' for a man is all.'

Snowy spat an epithet at the black-eyed man. 'Did I look like him the day you were lyin' out there, you bastard?'

Horn answered truthfully. 'It was the same black horse. You was a hell of a distance off. I didn't mean to hit anyone I didn't know. It was an accident, so help me, mister.'

Snowy lowered the gun a little, his face showing disgust and anger. 'I ought to kill you...Pick up those reins and start walkin' north up the creek...Give me just one little excuse, you son of a bitch, and I'll kill you yet!'

CHAPTER 10

ANSWERS

Bert brought Amos to the bunkhouse, where Snowy was watching their prisoner. When Amos filled the doorway, hunched forward and glaring, the black-eyed man looked back without a sound.

Amos went over close to the table where Bart Horn was sitting and balled up both fists. 'Talk,' he said in his gruff voice. 'If any of it's a lie we'll bury you out in the corral!'

Horn spoke quickly. 'I was ridin' over where your cattle are, north-west of here, and—'

Snowy cocked the hair-triggered six-gun. That deadly meshing of oily steel over oily steel stopped Bart Horn in mid-sentence, his eyes slid sideways to Snowy and the gun Snowy had aimed at Horn's chest.

'I was lookin' for some sign of a feller,' Horn said, starting over.

'The four of you,' snarled old Amos.

Horn dared not deny it after what he had said up along the creek, so he nodded his head. 'Me and some other fellers, yes.'

'Why?' snapped old Amos.

Horn's eyes flicked to the cocked six-gun then back again. 'He's maybe a fugitive from the law, mister.'

Without warning old Amos struck. Fifty years earlier he had probably been able to break a man's neck with a blow like that; as it was he knocked Bart Horn off the bench and along the floor, where Horn slammed up hard against the old iron wood-stove, and a cloud of dust and soot filtered downwards. He had trouble focusing his eyes. He also had difficulty jacking himself up by using both arms, but he had not lost consciousness.

The old man was thoroughly aroused and moved over, leaned to clasp a handful of shirt and lifted Horn to his feet with one hand. He pulled Horn toward the table and mercilessly slammed him back down upon the bench. He was breathing hard as he lowered his craggy old face to within inches of the stunned man's eyes and said, 'I warned you. We know why you're out here. Mister, one more time —and you're dead! Now, try again— what brought you fellers out here?'

Bart Horn raised his knuckles to the side of his mouth where the pain was. A flung-back trickle of blood was upon his cheek. He wiped it off and looked down at it. Bert thought old Amos was going to strike Horn again when the captive did not respond right away. Bert said, 'Give him a couple of minutes, Mister Northfield.'

Snowy growled at the old man. 'Leave him be.'

It required a full minute and a little more before Bart Horn shed the cobwebs in his brain. He wiped his torn mouth again, then fished for an old soiled bandanna to press it to the injury as he raised his eyes to the old man's face.

'There's a feller bringing pure gold to Morgansville and selling it. We followed him last time he was over there,' said the dazed man. 'We lost him a couple of times, but he was headin' this way.'

'And,' said Amos, 'you shot him.'

Bart Horn lowered the bandanna to reply. 'I didn't shoot him. I was far back.'

'Who did shoot him?' demanded old Amos.

Horn did not even hesitate before

replying. Evidently the look in the old man's eyes had convinced him that he really was very close to being killed. 'I don't know which feller did it. One is named Carl Young, the other feller is Jim Hazlitt. They rode ahead and set up an ambush. The feller rode right up into it, and when Carl and Jim jumped up to grab him, he drew on 'em. They said he was almighty fast. They shot him. That's all I know. That's the story they told when we met again. But the feller got clean away.'

'Where did you pick up his tracks again?' Amos growled.

'We found fresh shod-horse marks out yonder—up near the east end of this big meadow. There was no way to be sure, but we figured it had to belong to the man we wanted.'

Amos straightened up very slowly. 'How do you know he didn't ride on past, or go up into the mountains and ride around my place?'

Bart Horn dabbed at his swelling jaw and said, 'Mister—that's his black horse out yonder with your loose-stock.'

Amos turned toward the stove, and for as long as it took him to fill a cup with tepid coffee not a word was said. Horn continued to work his jaw, to feel it, and to use the bandanna to stop the slight trickle of blood from the side of his mouth where the lower lip had been torn.

Snowy went back to the door to lean there and examine the black-stocked Colt with the hair-trigger. It had been a commonplace sixgun at one time, but there was evidence that a skilled gunsmith had reworked it. Snowy eyed Bart Horn. Not many men spent money to have their sidearms customised— unless they were in a trade where that kind of weapon was indispensable.

Snowy said, 'About Hazlitt and Young—killers, are they?'

Horn's black stare lifted to Snowy's

face. 'Anyone'll kill when they got to,' he replied. 'Jim and Carl just try to get by like everyone else.'

Bert saw old Amos lower the cup and glare at Horn. He expected the big old man to attack the captive again. Instead he bitterly said, 'There's one feller you haven't named—who is he?'

'Buck Dillon,' replied Horn, raising the cloth to his mouth again.

Snowy's brows dropped and drew together. 'Dillon? Did he say he worked in this country?'

Horn nodded and lowered the cloth. 'Yeah. Used to ride all around the blue sage territory.' Horn was gazing at the soggy cloth in his hand when he also said, 'He told us, when he saw some of those chunks of gold this roan-haired feller brought in to sell, that there's supposed to be an old goldmine around this country somewhere.' Horn looked up again. 'That's why we followed the roan-haired feller. To see where he was gettin' that raw gold.'

Bert had a question for the prisoner. 'What do they plan to do?'

'Dillon knows the country. He's had us scoutin' all over here for a mine. All I've seen is some fat cattle—and three disagreeable fellows down on the blue sage prairie. One of them took a shot at me this morning. Hell, all I was doin' was circlin' far around their cattle to head northward up where you fellers met me.'

'Does Dillon know they took a shot at you?'

'No, how could he; I haven't seen anyone but you fellers since I left camp this morning to look around on the north range.'

Old Amos turned with a scornful remark and went to the door, where he turned, glared, then stamped out into the yard on his way to the main-house, no doubt to tell Rattlesnake what he had recently encountered at the bunkhouse.

Bart Horn glanced at Snowy. 'Now what?'

The older rangeman's answer indicated that Snowy at least was thinking ahead. He regarded the man with the discoloured, swelling jaw stonily as he answered. 'We're going to wait a spell, then all three of us are goin' down where you fellers have your camp.'

Bart Horn gazed steadily at Snowy for a long time, during which he said nothing. Then he looked away and raised the bandanna again. He did not comment but it was obvious from the look on his face that he did not think much of Snowy's suggestion.

Neither did Bert. Even with Horn out of it, the odds were not very good, and by the time he and Snowy could get into the area where the manhunters had their camp, the chances were going to have diminished still more, because by then the other three manhunters would have begun to suspect that something untoward had happened to Horn.

Bert rolled and lit a smoke, offered it to the captive, who shook his head, so Bert lit the smoke for himself, and did as old Amos had done, filled a dented tin cup with lukewarm coffee.

Snowy left the bunkhouse for a while. During his absence the black-eyed captive studied Bert, then said, 'You let me walk out that back door, and I'll give you a hundred dollars.'

Bert eyed the man, then tasted the coffee before answering. 'Do I look like an idiot?'

Horn answered quietly. 'Mister, I got the money in a belt under my shirt.'

'And you go back, then all four of you'd know enough to try bushwhacking again...You want a cup of cold coffee?'

'No thanks...That old man can hit like a kicking mule.'

Snowy returned with a length of chain

and two massive old padlocks. He did not say a word but went to work securing Bart Horn, and when the captive said, 'How do you expect me to ride my horse chained up like this,' Snowy yanked the loops still tighter without answering, and completed the trussing by snapping both those old padlocks into place.

Horn leaned to study the old locks. 'You sure you got a key? Those things look like they came over on the *Mayflower.*'

'Maybe they did,' stated Snowy. 'I think I got the key. At least I found one hangin' on a peg beside them.'

Horn looked up. 'Did you try it?'

Snowy hadn't. 'Hell no, what for? If you can't straddle the saddle we'll tie you over it like a sack of grain.'

Horn looked as though he thought Snowy Baker was not entirely sensible, then he nodded at Bert and said, 'I'd be right obliged for that cup of java now.'

Bert filled a cup and put it on the table near the captive. Horn tried to raise his arms, could not, so Snowy swore irritably but freed his arms so he could drink the coffee. Horn might as well have that, because as far as Snowy Baker was concerned he was not going to get anything else between now and the time they rode out.

There were not very many things Snowy did not like at all, but right up near the top of the list was bush-whackers, and perhaps because he had been the victim in this particular instance, he felt merciless toward Horn.

Bert closed the stove-damper to reduce the meagre fire to coals, then he went rummaging for something to eat while they waited for dusk. He did not like skulking around in the dark but evidently Snowy preferred it, and in this case it was probably the only way they could get up close enough to those other three manhunters to stand any chance at all against them in a fight—if there was a fight. It was obviously no accident that the manhunters had made their night-camp far out across open country.

Snowy, too, made a meal out of what he could find. He also went back for a few minutes, and when he returned he told Bert old Amos had been out there, and had said for Snowy and Bert to be almighty careful because, dark or no dark, men like Horn was riding with were as dangerous as side-winders.

Bert finished his coffee, all but the dregs, which were too bitter, then he cast a sardonic look in Baker's direction, but he kept silent. If there was one thing he had not needed since his first run-in down here in the blue sage country, it was an admonition to be careful.

CHAPTER 11

FIRELIGHT

They left the yard just short of dusk, which Snowy did not approve of because he thought Bart Horn's friends might still be out there watching, but the need to be down where they could see open country before full dark arrived was important, too.

Old Amos watched them leave the yard from his porch. He was understandably anxious. Except for the wounded outlaw he would have harnessed a team and driven a wagon to accompany Bert and Snowy, but leaving Rattlesnake alone in his feeble condition was unthinkable, so Amos simply stood up there and watched the riders until they were lost to sight in the late evening, then went dourly back inside.

It was a warm evening. Most of the recent evenings had been warm. In fact this time of year the nights frequently remained warm until past midnight.

If there was to be a moon there was no evidence of it yet, and although the stars were up there, they were pale in a sky which was sooty but not dark yet as the riders went directly eastward up the Northfield meadow.

Bart Horn was astride; Snowy had relented at the last moment and left Horn's legs unchained, but he still had the man's wrists secured.

Horn's swollen jaw lent his face a lop-sided appearance, but he did not seem to be in any particular pain. When Bert asked if he wanted a smoke Horn answered with a slight slur which was probably caused by the swelling in his lower face.

'Don't smoke much. Thanks all the same.'

They began angling southward so as to ride up the long, gradual slope between the meadow and the rougher country to southward. By then if anyone saw them he would have to be very close, close enough for them to see him, and Snowy, who was watching for something like this, seemed satisfied that there was no one close by.

Bert topped out first, and drew rein for as long as was required to search the gradually increasing darkness for firelight.

It was out there, in the same place it had been the previous night. Snowy leaned on his saddlehorn for thoughtful moments before speaking. 'Horn, we're goin' to use you to get up close.'

The bushwhacker mumbled his answer to that. 'I figured it had to be something like that.'

Snowy spoke again as though Horn had remained silent. 'We're goin' to be directly behind you when we walk down there. You want to remember that—me behind you with the hair-triggered gun.'

Horn was sitting gazing far out where the firelight was when he said, 'I guess you know you're goin' to get all three of us killed.'

Snowy did not reply. He eased back in the saddle and turned slightly as he led off in the direction he and Bert had ridden the night when Snowy had scouted up the camp of the manhunters.

There were no trees down there but Bert found a number of flourishing big clumps of brush where they could anchor the horses, and here, finally, Snowy unlocked the big old brass padlock which secured Horn's arms. As he draped the chain from a bush he said, 'Once more, bushwhacker—I'll be directly behind you.'

Horn looked from the distant campfire to his captors. 'You figure me to walk down there into camp?'

Snowy smiled. 'Yeah. After that it'll be up to your friends.'

Horn spat and raised a hand to gently feel his swollen jaw. 'You'll never get it done, mister, not in a million years. You don't know the men you're goin' up against.'

Snowy made a curt gesture. 'Start walkin' and no more talk.'

Bart Horn walked. Bert was slightly to Horn's left, Snowy was slightly to his right. They could watch the firelight and their hostage at the same time. Bert, impressed by Horn's solemn prediction, palmed his sixgun and cocked it while they were still a considerable distance out.

Darkness was settling, visibility was diminishing to a few yards, and by the time the aromatic scent of a campfire was discernible, there was a little moon coming from behind invisible mountain rims.

The land was silent. It was inhabited by a number of nocturnal creatures, but between the heavy man-scent and that campfire down yonder, the varmints were unwilling to forage and were lying close in their nests, nervously testing the air.

Bert was eventually able to make out two men hunched at the fire eating. He sought the third manhunter but could not locate him. He moved close to Snowy and said they had better halt where they were. Snowy touched Bart Horn and gave an order, then the three of them stood out in the night without speaking until Snowy was satisfied that there was indeed one man missing. His brow furrowed, he turned and looked back, then he looked elsewhere before softly saying, 'Stay here, Bert,' and left him and the bushwhacker as he went ahead alone.

Horn revealed knowledge of this sort of thing by saying, 'He's goin' to count the horses.'

Horn was correct. When Snowy returned he nodded at Bert. 'They're all down there now. I figured that one had to be, because their horses are on this side of the camp, all three of 'em.'

Bert wanted to know how close Snowy had got, so he asked if his partner had heard the manhunters talking. Snowy hadn't because he had not got any closer than the horses.

Horn sighed audibly when Snowy growled at him to start walking again. He did not take his eyes off the campfire and he did not say a word as they went still closer, went down almost to the place where three hobbled horses were nibbling at grass-stalks amid the crumbling granite.

When they halted this time, the feeling of crisis intensified. All three manhunters were visible through the night. They were too far distant for features to be made out, but they were eating and seemed relaxed. Bart Horn shook his head, but did not speak, so neither of his captors knew what that meant, nor, at this point, did they care.

Bert stepped up beside Snowy to say, 'Horn can walk directly down to them from here. You and I'd better fan out far to the left and right, so's we'll have 'em covered from two sides.'

Snowy nodded. He may have been considering some such disposition himself, but now as he stepped up beside Bart Horn he said only what he wanted the captive to do.

'Walk down a ways, then sing out. Tell 'em your horse broke a leg up north, where we caught you, and you been walkin' ever since.'

It was at least possible. Horn did not acknowledge that he had heard, but when Snowy nudged him with his own gun, the bushwhacker turned to face the older man, his features pale and evil in the poor light.

'You'd do better just to stampede their horses.'

Horn might have been correct; setting someone afoot in country like this made them helpless. But it also left them armed and deadly. It would also make these particular men realise that since hobbled horses could not release themselves, they had enemies close by, and Horn had already intimated how dangerous his friends were.

Snowy punched Horn in the ribs with the pistol barrel. 'Walk! and be damned careful!'

Horn put a sardonic look upon Snowy Baker, then strolled ahead. There was no way to be careful under these circumstances, the best a man could do was try not to end up dead any way he could think to accomplish it.

Bert and Snowy exchanged a nod as soon as Bart Horn passed the horses, then turned in opposite directions and began a circling stalk in the direction of the firelight.

Bert's gun-palm was wet. He shifted the cocked Colt to his other hand, dried his palm down the outer seam of his trousers, then regripped the gun. He could have shot all three of those man-hunters around the fire, and if he had been Bart Horn he probably would have. There were disadvantages of having a conscience, to having grown up believing in a code of conduct which considered bushwhacking to · be the most unforgivable of all range-country crimes.

He was alone on the left side of the firelight, advancing very carefully until he was satisfied he was in excellent handgun range, then he sank to one knee to wait.

Snowy had to be on the west side somewhere. Bart Horn was faintly visible to Bert as he finally paused to call ahead. 'Hey; save some of that grub for me!'

Instantly three men sprang up and stepped away from the firelight. Horn called again. 'Damned horse broke his leg a hell of a ways north of that old ranch-yard.'

Finally, one of the men down by the camp called back. 'You been walkin' all this time?'

Horn answered less loudly as he began covering the last hundred or so yards. 'Well, I sure as hell haven't been riding.'

The manhunters eased up slightly, went back closer to the fire. One of them said, 'Jim, dash up some of that grub,' then the same man spoke to Bart Horn. 'Did you find anythin' up there?'

Horn was getting closer as he replied. 'Yeah. Some nice fat cattle on the north range of that old man's place.'

A different voice spoke out annoyedly. 'Cattle, hell; maybe some day we'll come back for them. What about the feller with the roan hair?'

Bart Horn was less than thirty yards

from his friends when he answered this time. 'He's there sure as hell. That old bastard who owns the place's likely got him in the main-house.'

The irritable voice came right back, 'Did you *see* him?'

Horn answered shortly. 'No, I didn't see him. How the hell was I goin' to get into the house? What did you fellers find?'

The first man to speak, the one with authority to his words, said, 'You stay in camp, Bart. We'll go over there. If he's in the house we'll find him. Or if that old man knows anything we'll shove his bare feet into the stove until he talks.'

Horn was less than thirty feet away now when he said, 'Bring me back a horse,' then he suddenly hurled himself ahead to the ground and yelled. '*They're around you!*'

Bert had been awaiting Snowy's command for the three armed manhunters to freeze in place. Maybe Bart Horn had been expecting that too, but if Snowy had been about to call out, his opportunity was gone now.

The three armed men sprang away to get clear of the backgrounding firelight, and from the west Snowy snapped off a shot which missed the man he was trying to hit in mid-jump, and the slug struck squarely into the campfire. Sparks, bits of flaming wood, ash and dirt exploded in all directions.

Someone fired back at Snowy's muzzleblast, and Bert saw his man dimly silhouetted as he whirled in a crouch. Bert fired and the manhunter went down in a sprawling heap, then began to furiously roll away from the firelight. Someone fired at Bert's muzzleblast, and came very close because Bart had not moved after firing, instinct should have warned him to do. He did move, after that close call, but someone in the vicinity of the campfire had either heard him or seen him because two rapid gunshots flamed in the night and one bullet, aimed low, flung sharp little stones into Bart's legs as he drove ahead and pressed flat while whipping up his sixgun.

Bart Horn was no longer on the ground near the firelight. Bert did not waste much time trying to locate him until someone over amid the tangle of camp and horse equipment blazed away in Snowy's direction with a carbine.

Bert was holding his gun to fire in that direction when a man suddenly rose up to one knee not a hundred feet away and swung his sixgun to bear. Bert frantically kicked dirt in an effort to get away. The man fired, dirt and dust hit Bert in the face as he fired back, then frantically rolled again.

The kneeling man dropped down and did not fire again, but Horn was still trying to find Snowy with the carbine, and Bert's eyes were flooded with water so he could not come to Snowy's aid.

When Bert fished out his bandanna to desperately try and clear the water from his burning eyes, someone, perhaps the kneeling man, yelled out exultantly to his companions. 'I got this son of a bitch over here!'

The manhunters now turned toward the area Snowy Baker had fired from. Bert mopped frantically, then cursed, dropped the bandanna and fired at a moving figure crossing toward the west side of the smoking, less brilliant fire. The silhouette half turned in surprise, then buckled at the knees and fell.

Snowy was no longer firing. Bert blinked furiously as good vision began to return, and now there was an interlude of silence. Bert rolled still farther southward, fetched up behind a wiry sage bush and hurriedly punched out spent casings and jammed in fresh loads. He was finishing when the carbine fired again, twice very fast, and from the west a sixgun blazed back.

Bert eased up to look. He could see no one. He crawled around the sage bush, and came almost face to face with a beard-stubbled, hatless man, who was also crawling. For two seconds they stared at one another, then the stranger dropped down, rolled, and snapped off a wild shot.

Bert did not drop down. He tracked the rolling man, and fired when the stranger stopped moving. The man was punched savagely several feet over the flinty ground, and did not move again.

Bert hung there watching the man he had shot. There was no sign of life, so he started down past the dead man to go around the southern end of the campfire in Snowy's direction, and was midway past the firelight when someone out to the west tried a sound-shot.

Dirt flew a yard to Bert's left, up in the direction of the fire. Bert rolled away and made no further attempt to reach Snowy Baker.

At the same time the man with the carbine fired in the direction of the muzzleblast which had sent the slug toward Bert. He got an answering shot which was so close to the carbine shot it sounded like a continuation of the same noise.

Now there was a second interlude of silence. Bert guessed the man with the carbine had shot out his weapon. For a while he lay without moving, but as the silence drew out taut, he gingerly dried his eyes with a soiled cuff and raised up slightly trying to see a man-shape.

Someone was coming toward him from around the left of the fire. He could not see who it was but could make out the soft, abrasive sound of bootleather over crumbly earth.

Bert pressed flat, swivelled his body the way a lizard would have done, raised his sixgun and held the thumbpad atop his gun-hammer, and waited.

The man was holding a carbine two-handedly across his body and he was creeping as soundlessly as he could, to pass Bert to the east. He was out of the firelight, which was no longer bright, but that belated moon and all those high stars showed the man as a ghostly shadow.

Bert had no idea who the man was, but he *did* know that it was not Snowy Baker; the oncoming man was too tall. Bert cocked the gun. Instantly the silhouette swung his carbine and fired blind. Bert did not fire blind. When he squeezed off his shot the silhouette flung his saddlegun sideways, flung both arms wide, and went down backwards.

Now the silence closed in and remained.

Bert dried his burning eyes again, and waited. He was prepared to lie out there and wait until daylight, if that proved necessary.

Ten full minutes passed before there

was a sound, then a voice called from the south-west. 'Bert?'

For a while Osborne did not answer, not until he realised that only one man among the manhunters had known his name, and he was sure he had shot that man when he had come sneaking southward with a carbine.

He called back. 'Snowy?'

'Yeah. You all right?'

Bert let his breath go in a shaky sigh. 'Just fine. Can't see worth a damn, scairt pea-green, not sure I can stand up—but, yeah. I'm just fine. You?'

'Gawddamned scorpion bit me,' answered Snowy Baker, 'and one of those bastards shot the heel off my boot and cracked my ankle, but otherwise I never felt better...Are any of 'em alive?'

Bert did not know. 'They aren't shootin' at us,' he said. 'That ought to mean something. Why don't you stand up and we'll find out.'

'Go to hell!'

CHAPTER 12

TOWARD DAWN

When Bert and Snowy came together below the havoc which had been the manhunters' camp, they heard a distant horse suddenly break away to the east in a belly-down run, and for as long as they could distinguish that sound they stood down there in silence. Then Bert said, 'One of 'em didn't get hurt too bad.'

Snowy's retort to that was tart. 'Damned wonder anyone did, in the dark.'

They went over to the man Bert had shot, who had been carrying the carbine, and Snowy leaned to look, then straightened back with a wag of his head. 'The damned fool. All he had to do was walk up to them, but he had to yell a warning.'

Bert only glanced at his victim and turned toward the dying fire as he said, 'At least we know that one's name.'

There were two dead men about thirty feet apart upon the north side of the camp, one of them was that man Bert had crawled around the bush to meet face to face. The other one was facing west and had been hit by a sixgun slug high in the body.

Bert went over where the horse equipment was lying, pulled someone's saddle around, propped it up and sat on the cantle as he used his shirt-tail to drain off excess water from his eyes, and to afterwards roll and light a smoke with hands that were not quite steady.

What he really needed was a jolt of rye whiskey, but he made no effort to search for a bottle, although there probably was one somewhere around.

Snowy came over, limping, and sat down also. Neither of them had anything to say for a long while, then Snowy arose and limped around searching saddle-bags and bedrolls until he found what he sought, and limped back to offer Bert the first drink.

The whiskey burned all the way down, but Bert began to feel better, and a half-hour later he volunteered to go out and bring their horses to the camp, so Snowy would not have to walk out there.

The night was as silent now as it had been before the fight; perhaps more silent because any four-legged creatures who might have been bold enough to risk foraging despite the man-scent, before the gun battle, were no longer within miles of the campsite.

Bert mounted his horse and led Snowy's animal back. When they were ready to leave camp they freed the remaining pair of hobbled horses, turned the animal Bart Horn had ridden in the direction of the home-place, and drove all three horses ahead of them. The manhunters' horses followed the lead of the Mexican Hat horse, and since neither of the riders behind them made any effort to push them, the loose-stock went along docilely, as though they knew where they were heading.

It was a long ride in almost total silence. Snowy's painful ankle caused him anguish and for most of the distance he rode with that foot out of the stirrup. When they eventually reached the dark yard, a chill was coming into the late night. Snowy turned his horse so that he could lean down from the saddle to grip the hitchrack, and eased off, so that he did not have to put his sore leg to the ground.

Bert took care of the saddled animals and allowed the loose-stock to go on past the barn and out upon the west side of Northfield's meadow. Then he helped Snowy to the bunkhouse, lit the lantern, fired up the stove, and watched as Snowy worked his heel-less boot off over the swollen ankle—with considerable profanity.

Bert looked at the ankle. This was something he knew about. He offered to wrap it and Snowy hoisted the leg atop a horseshoe keg beside his bunk and Bert went to work. He first wrapped the instep of Snowy's foot, then, with that tightly supported, he began to bandage the ankle. He made that bandage fairly tight as well. When he was finished Snowy said, 'I'll be damned. It don't hurt.'

Bert heated coffee atop the wood-stove and watched Baker ease the injured leg to the floor. He knew what was going to happen but he also knew that telling Snowy in advance would be like trying to reason with a stone wall. Snowy leaned, felt almost no pain, then leaned a little more, felt slightly more pain, and was going to arise to test the ankle when he saw Bert's face, and said, 'Hadn't ought to stand on it, eh?'

'Sure; stand on it if you like. But if you like to hurt yourself, why not just take the stove poker and hit yourself over the head with it; at least that won't hurt your ankle.'

Snowy leaned back. 'I never had a sprung ankle before.'

Bert was filling two cups with coffee when he replied. 'You got one now.'

'When can I ride?'

'Tomorrow,' stated Bert, carrying a cup to Snowy on his bunk. 'It's your ankle got hurt, not your butt. The only thing you won't be able to do very well for a week or two is walk.'

Snowy tasted the coffee. It was as bitter as original sin. 'I never walk anyway,' he told Bert. 'That's why the Lord give a horse four big legs and a tiny brain, and he gave me a bigger brain an' only two legs.' Snowy drank the coffee without a grimace. 'We're supposed to go down an' help those free-grazers move their cattle tomorrow.'

Bert sank down over at the table, pitched his hat aside and tasted the coffee. What it needed was whiskey. He said, 'Yeah, I know—but there aren't any rustlers left. At least there aren't any fellers the free-grazers believe are rustlers, left.'

'We'd ought to ride down there, anyway.'

Bert sighed and felt his sore eyes. 'First, Snowy, we got to take the old man's wagon, some tools, and go down and bury those fellers.'

'I don't figure my ankle'll be up to it,' Snowy exclaimed, avoiding Bert Osborne's steady gaze. Then he also said with more honesty, 'I never liked diggin' holes to put people into.'

'Who does like it?'

Snowy sighed. 'Yeah. All right.' He

rolled up on to his side with his back to Bert and composed himself for sleep. Bert finished the coffee, turned down the stove damper, then instead of bedding down right away, went out and stood a while in the cooling night, studying the stars and the lazy old moon.

When he eventually went back inside to his bunk, and got under the blankets, he could not sleep. He still saw crouching man-shapes limned feebly by a ruined campfire, and could still hear gunshots and see the savage muzzle-blasts they made.

Some men, like Snowy Baker, could turn in under these circumstances knowing only that they were exhausted, injured, and dead tired, while other men did not think about the tiredness or the exhaustion, or even the salvation which had kept them alive while other men died around them; that kind of a man took a long time to recover from the kind of ordeal Bert Osborne had survived, and if they'd ever had doubts about the validity of what they had done, and the correctness of the cause in which they had done it, they did not recover at all.

Bert finally slept, but by the time his body demanded sleep it was so close to dawn that what rest he got was nowhere nearly enough. But he was young, and that made all the difference in the world when Snowy whistled him out of a deep sleep. He sat up, felt his stubbly jaw, and piled out of bed without even noticing that Snowy was hobbling about with one boot on, and with his other foot bootless and expertly bandaged.

Amos came down across the yard before daybreak, attracted by the bunkhouse stovepipe giving off a fine head of smoke. He saw Snowy, who was making their meagre breakfast, but because Bert was out back shaving, Amos went to lean on the big old bunkhouse table, looking anxious as he said, 'Where's your sidekick?'

'At the wash-rack. Don't worry, he didn't get shot.'

'What's wrong with your foot.'

'Bullet hit my boot-heel last night, taken it plumb off and wrenched hell out of my ankle,' stated Snowy, and having delivered himself of that, he also said, 'One got away. We're goin' down in the wagon after we eat to bury the others.'

Amos's brows jumped up. 'All of them?'

Snowy frowned at the big old man. 'It wasn't an army. There was only four. One got away after the fight on a horse, ridin' east…The other three—are dead.'

'That feller you captured too?'

'Yes. He bought in on their side…You want some fried meat and coffee?'

'No,' replied the old man, straightening. 'No, thanks,' Then he said, 'I'll go along and help bury them. With them gone Rattlesnake won't need me—for a while, anyway.'

Snowy did not want Northfield along. 'Stay with him,' he said. 'A feller in his condition needs constant watching... How is he?'

'Walking last evening. From his bed to the outhouse and back.'

'That's good, Amos. That's *damned* good in fact. I would have bet money I'd be one of his pallbearers.'

'Wants to leave,' Amos said, and dropped his thick brows in a frown. 'Wants to saddle up and head on down to California. He's got a little place down there—in some place called Hungry Holler.'

Snowy considered that, then wagged his head. 'The name don't make me want to go out there.'

'Well, he said that between tryin' to find decent water and a vein o' gold he figures is under some rocks out there, he's dead set on headin' out as soon as he can.'

Snowy slid the pair of old tin plates atop the table and poured coffee too, then he looked at Amos. 'Hell, he won't be able to ride for a month.'

Before departing, Amos agreed, but he also said, 'You don't know Rattlesnake like I do. He's pig-headed. He'll go when he figures he's got to...About those dead fellers...'

'We'll fetch back their outfits and all,' stated Baker. 'We'll pile plenty of rocks atop the graves. Maybe the one who escaped'll come back with the law and we give him their property.'

Amos nodded and went to the door, ducked through on his way to the mainhouse to tell Rattlesnake the manhunters who had tried to capture him were dead; that only one got away alive and he was riding fast when he left the country, and when Bert came in from out back to eat, Snowy eased down with his sore ankle shoved gingerly under the table, and said, 'The free-grazers sure as hell heard the fight last night.'

Bert was not interested in speculations. 'They'd have to be deaf not to have heard it. What horses do we hitch to that old wagon in the shed?'

'I'll show you directly, right now I'm eating.'

'Do you know where the digging tools are?'

'Yes.'

'Then let's be on our way,' said Bert, arising as he drained his tin cup.

Snowy looked up irritably. 'I'm not through eatin', darn it all. Those fellers aren't goin' anywhere. Just take your time.'

Bert watched his partner stab meat for a moment, then walked out of the bunkhouse in the direction of the wagonshed. He could at least pull the rig out where they'd hitch horses to it. Anything was preferable to watching Snowy sit in there and eat like a hog after what had happened last night.

CHAPTER 13

AFTER THE SMOKE CLEARED

It took hours to get back down by wagon to the silent, wrecked camp of the manhunters. It took more hours to dig the graves, especially since Snowy, despite a dogged willingness to help, was seriously handicapped by his injured ankle.

The sun was high and slanting off towards the west when they finally pitched the last of the private effects of the manhunters into the old wagon, then sat down to rest—and saw horsemen approaching from the west, coming across the blue sage prairie without haste, even with a noticeable lack of haste. Snowy tipped ash from his smoke and said, 'Moran an' his partners...I'm not surprised. It's a wonder they didn't show up earlier.'

He was at least right about the identity of the riders, who rode bunched up for the last mile or so, occasionally speaking among themselves as they made out three graves, freshly mounded.

Bert was comfortable in the wagon-shade. His arms ached mildly from the digging and his hands, which were more accustomed to leather and lariat-rope than to crowbar and shovel handles, were not as sore as they would be this evening. Until Moran and his companions saw the two seated and relaxed figures in the shade of the wagon, recognising both Snowy and Bert, they did not appear entirely willing to cover the last couple of hundred yards, then Wood Kendall raised his left arm in a high greeting, and Bert returned the salutation, after which the free-grazers came steadily on.

They halted and looked at the scattered firebrands, dead cold now and black. They saw other vestiges of the furious battle, studied the side-by-side graves, then Moran gazed at the seated men and said, 'Must have been quite a ruckus.'

Snowy answered. 'It was, an' you fellers must have heard it.'

Moran nodded, then looked at the equipment in the wagon. 'Where's the fourth one?'

'Got away,' stated Snowy, and sat waiting the next question.

Wood Kendall asked it. 'How did it happen?'

'We caught one scoutin' up North-field cattle north-west—up above the ranch—and caught him hands down. Then we used him to get in close to this here camp—and after that there was a fight.'

Wesley Moran considered the pair of seated men. 'Just the two of you?'

Snowy sighed because he was tiring of this. 'Yeah, just the two of us.'

'And you got hurt in the foot?'

'Ankle,' replied Snowy, and changed the subject. 'We'll be a little late gettin' down to help you gather cattle. Likely won't be down until in the morning, if that's all right with you.'

Moran nodded. 'Sure; whenever you show up.' He seemed to be regarding Baker and Osborne differently now. Dave, too, although he had the best reason for still being hostile, seemed to regard the pair of sweaty, unsmiling seated men in wagon-shade, differently.

Bert said, 'You moved your camp yet?'

Moran shifted slightly in the saddle. 'We're goin' to as soon as we get back... Except for the shade and the piddlin' creek it's not a good place anyway; the horses darn near fell into that brush

212

crevice. We had to tie ropes together and string them across the front of it to keep 'em out of there. Dave found a better place about a mile on westerly.' Moran glanced again at the graves, then lifted his rein-hand. 'You boys need any help?'

Snowy looked up at Wesley Moran. 'Not today,' he said, and turned to gingerly arise.

The free-grazers turned westerly and rode close-bunched and talking as they went back to the territory where they had their cattle and their camp.

Bert helped Snowy climb to the driver's side of the wagon. They started back for the meadow with Bert drinking deeply from the canteen under the seat, and Snowy looking thoughtful. He eventually said. 'You know what I think; they got us figured as ring-tailed roarers. They think we came down here, just the pair of us, an' attacked those four fellers.'

'We did,' said Bert.

Snowy shook his head. 'What I had in mind was to take 'em without a fight. That's why I wanted that darned fool Bart Horn to get their attention...No one in his right mind would tackle men like that with odds of two to one.'

Bert spat over the side of the creaking, groaning old wagon. 'It sure as hell wasn't my idea to fight 'em, but it happened, so let the free-grazers think what they want...Hey, Snowy; what's the point of us helpin' them bring in their cattle?'

Baker nodded. This had occurred to him back at the manhunters' camp. With the pseudo cattle-thieves dead or dispersed there was no need for the free-grazers to bunch their herd so it would be easier to keep an eye on. But Snowy was thinking along a different tangent.

'I can't walk worth a darn, and settin' around the yard don't appeal to me, so might as well go down and ride a little, hadn't we?'

Bert did not look at the older man, he slowly and with meticulous care built a fine example of a hand-rolled brown-paper cigarette, lit it, and blew smoke at the pale, brassy sky, and finally swung a sidelong glance at his companion. He had come to know Snowy Baker reasonably well over the past few weeks. Better, in fact, than Snowy would have believed.

He said, 'You don't want to ride under a hot sun in the stinkin' dust of a bunch of wild darned cattle just for the hell of it.'

Snowy did not answer until he had helped the team up a low, gradual grade which terminated atop the higher landswell which formed the southern barrier of Northfield's meadow. Like most men who drove teams up hills, Snowy not only slackened the lines so the animals could get their heads down, but he also leaned far forward. When they were atop the broad rim and Snowy sat back as the horses began their descent on the far side, and hoisted his booted foot to the brake-shoe to skid the rear wheels if it became necessary, in order to keep the wagon from riding up on to the horse's hocks, he said, 'What other reason would I have?'

Bert's reply was blunt. 'That damned mine.'

Snowy offered no refutation. They were nearly down the slope to open meadow when he answered. 'It's around here somewhere, Bert.'

'It belongs to the old man, Snowy.'

'Well, hell, I didn't say I was goin' to jump it, did I?'

Bert flicked ash. 'I wouldn't let you if you tried.'

Snowy turned a pained look upon his companion. 'I just want to see it is all. I've heard of it since I first came into this country. No one knew where it was, but they sure had some tall stories to tell about it. What's wrong with a man just seein' it?'

'Nothing,' stated Bert, and pitched his dead cigarette over the wagon-side, 'but I've heard stories too.'

'About the lost Spanish mine?'

'No. About how some pretty decent fellers go crazy when they see a vein of gold.'

Snowy turned his pained expression forward as he put slight pressure on the near-side line so as to bring the team on a gradual westward course. 'Ah, hell,' he muttered in obvious disgust. 'Bert, I never had anything and at my age I'm used to it. If I found enough gold to make me rich you know what I'd likely do? Go set in a town and commence drinkin' and chasin' dancin' girls, and sleepin' up off the ground, and maybe even eatin' three big, fine meals a day, and get a heart ailment and be dead in a couple of years.'

Bert tipped down his hat because the

sun was getting lower now and bothering his sensitive eyes. He leaned against the board at his back, hooked both thumbs in his shellbelt and sighed. 'And playin' cards in a cool saloon; maybe get into some business like buyin' and sellin' cattle; maybe buy four or five breedy horses like that black gelding Rattlesnake's got.'

'Yeah. Maybe do those things too.'

'Snowy, you ever been out to San Francisco in California? I knew a rider up in Montana one time who'd been out there. He said a man'd ought to see that town if he never sees any other place, before he dies.'

'Well, yeah. Maybe go out there too.'

Bert tipped his hat lower and was quiet for a while. Then he said, 'Not on your damned life,' and neither of them had anything more to say until they reached the yard, put up the team, and were leaning on the wagon-tongue to push the wagon back into its shed. Then

Bert said, 'But I'll tell you something. With Rattlesnake flat on his back, someone's got to pack those pouches of gold out of the blue sage country and turn 'em into money.'

It was hot. Inside the wagon-shed there was not a breath of air. They leaned on the wagon to catch their breath and mopped off sweat. Snowy hoisted his bandaged, soiled foot to the tongue and looked out to where the meadow ran eastward for a considerable distance. There was nothing out there but some heat waves.

Snowy did not offer a comment on Bert's suggestion. Mainly because Bert had trapped him once, while they were approaching the yard, and he was not going to be trapped twice in the same day.

Bert straightened up finally, because he was thirsty. 'I guess gold gets into a man's blood, no matter how old he is, eh?'

Snowy answered because he knew what his partner was thinking. 'Yeah, I expect so. An' what does an old gaffer do with either bags of gold or the money it brings him? He sets in his house and knows how rich he is while he listens to his arteries hardenin' and feels the lead gettin' heavier in his rear. Then he dies, and it ain't possible to carry the money with you, is it?'

Bert pushed off sweat with a shirt-cuff and started out of the shed in the direction of the bunkhouse. Snowy limped in his wake.

They washed out back, Snowy got Bert to make him a fresh bandage to replace the one which had nearly worn through from being walked on. They were ready to bed down early because it had been a hell of a day and neither of them had had enough rest the night before, and old Amos came barging in, making enough noise to rouse the dead.

He had to know every detail, so they

made coffee and told him what they had done, told him about the equipment still in the wagon, explained that they were going down in the morning to help the free-grazers, and when it was all out in the open Bert asked about Rattlesnake.

Amos drummed atop the table. He had clearly been bothered by some deep thoughts during their absence. Because he usually wore a scowl that aspect of his present expression did not have to mean very much as Bert and Snowy waited.

'Rattlesnake's perkin' up more every day. I'd guess maybe in another couple weeks he'll be ready to ride...' The old man peered first at Bert then at Snowy before continuing. 'He's got a hell of a distance to go; across Arizona after he gets out of New Mexico...And it's goin' to be hot from here on...'

Snowy got some coffee to mask his impatience. Bert filled two cups and put one at Northfield's elbow and took the

221

second cup back to the bench where he had been sitting.

Old Amos abruptly arose and stalked to the door. 'We'll talk tomorrow when you get back from down yonder,' he said, and closed the bunkhouse door after himself. Snowy promptly hitched over and opened the door. It had been open before Amos had arrived, to catch any stray breeze which might enter the yard. As he turned back Snowy said, 'Crazy as a loon.'

Bert had never yielded to this point and did not do so now. 'He's no more cazy than you are.'

'He sure didn't make any sense just now!'

Bert drained his cup before replying. 'He's bothered by something, that's all.'

Snowy did not press it. He limped to the table, finished his coffee and finally suggested that they go down to the shed and paw through the belongings of those defunct manhunters.

In the yard, where heat was rising from the hardpan earth, there was a little breeze which made things bearable, but inside the wagon-shed the heat was not alleviated at all as they lowered the tail-gate and considered the saddlery, bedrolls, the saddlebags and weapons.

They were just beginning to examine what was in the wagon when a horse whinnied from somewhere north and west of the yard. They went out to where they could see in that direction, noticed several horses less than a half-mile from the back of the barn, standing stock-still, with their heads up, pointing.

Back in front of the barn they saw a solitary rider coming down the broad meadow from the east. He was making no attempt to avoid being seen, and the closer he got the more obvious it became that he knew where he was going. It was also obvious that he was not a free-grazer.

Bert squinted then said, 'Badge on

his shirtfront.'

Snowy groaned. 'You go tell Amos, I'll meet him out here.'

As Bert started across the yard, though, old Amos stepped out on to his veranda. How he had spied the stranger he never said, nor did it matter, but as Bert reached the steps Amos said, 'Lawman, isn't he?'

Bert nodded, wondering how the old man had been able to make that out when he consistently complained that his eyesight was failing.

Amos dropped his gaze to Bert. 'We'll talk to him down at the barn. He's not to come inside this house.'

Snowy was leaning on the tie-rack when Bert and the old man got down there. The oncoming rider was close enough now to be able to make out that three armed men were lounging out front of the barn in the afternoon shade. He entered the yard at a steady walk, riding purposefully on a loose rein, did not raise a hand or heed the waiting men until he had made a visual study of the yard, all the buildings, and finally the barn-area, then he eased over and halted a few yards off, and nodded.

He was a leathery-faced, thin-lipped, cold-eyed man with a sprinkling of grey at both temples. He had a carbine in the boot under his right leg and an ivory-stocked Colt tied to his right leg. He could have been forty or sixty, it was impossible to tell, but one thing about him was clear enough: he was not a man to be taken lightly.

When Amos did not say it, Bert did. Get down, mister. There's water out back.'

The rider dismounted, still without showing anything of his face, and tugged off his riding-gloves while he made his appraisal of the three men facing him. 'My name is Frank Archer —deputy US marshal out of Denver.' He did not ask the names of Bert,

Snowy or Amos Northfield, and in fact he did not allow them the time to introduce themselves. 'I've got some warrants.' As Marshal Archer said this he delved in a pocket and brought out several folded papers, which he very methodically unfolded and spread out. 'See anyone here you recognise?' he asked.

Old Amos's fierce scowl deepened. He recognised one face. Snowy and Bert recognised all four faces. Snowy said, 'Yeah; those first three are dead. We buried 'em this morning, early. That fourth feller got away.' At the stare he was getting from the federal lawman, Snowy elaborated. 'They were scoutin' up cattle when Bert here and I caught one—that one; Bart Horn—then we rode out to their camp about eight miles from here. That was last night...There was a fight. This morning we went back and buried those three, and that feller got out to the horses and rode like hell goin' eastward.'

Marshall Archer continued to hold the wanted posters out and to gaze steadily at Snowy Baker. 'You're sure it was these four?'

Snowy reddened. 'You want to go dig 'em up and look for yourself?'

Marshal Archer folded his dodgers, pocketed them and loosened a little as he said, 'I got to, I guess.'

Snowy was still annoyed so he said, 'I'll draw you a map, but I'm not goin' back down there.'

Marshal Archer stood briefly in thought, then said, 'There's rewards for those four. Cattle-thievin', stage robbin' and two suspected murders in Southern Colorado. If you want to put in a claim you'd ought to ride down there with me.'

Snowy was adamant. 'I don't care how much reward there is, I'm not goin' back down there,' he said, giving the lawman look for look.

Archer turned to Amos, whose fierce expression was all the answer he required, then he glanced at Bert, who said, 'I don't need money bad enough to take that kind, Marshal.'

Frank Archer shrugged. 'I'll need a map,' he said, and Snowy knelt to begin drawing in the dust. Marshal Archer would have no difficulty in finding the graves once he topped out upon that landswell which offered a view of the char where the campfire had been, and Snowy went over it several times until Marshal Archer nodded fully understanding of where to ride along the landswell in sight of the char and the fresh graves.

He did not tarry. Did not even water his horse, which Amos growled about after the lawman had ridden out of the yard. Bert was more relieved than annoyed. He had been certain the lawman had had a dodger on Rattlesnake Rowe, and Archer had not even mentioned the fugitive over at the main-house.

CHAPTER 14

A HOT DAY OF SUMMER

In the morning they rode down to the blue sage prairie, found the cattle without difficulty even though they were mostly to the south and west, scattered out for miles, and rode to the broad arroyo where the camp had been, then picked up shod-horse sign and followed it along the crumbly northward country-side, where there was no other sign, and found the camp upon a low, broad rib of curving land, where there were three old trees and, at the lower part of the swell, a tributary of the same creek which had watered the area around the first camp.

first camp.

Dave was there alone. He offered a tentative smile and said Moran and Kendall had already struck out southward to bring the widest drift in closer. Then he got his mount and struck out back eastward, talking as they rode along.

Dave was different. The belligerence which he had consistently showed was gone. He seemed to accept Baker and Osborne the same way he had accepted the other pair of older men, Moran and Kendall. The longer Bert rode with him, listened to him and watched him, the more he got the impression that the powerfully built, bull-necked rangeman was one of those men, by no means rare on the frontier, who because of some lack within themselves, felt impelled to attract attention by being truculent.

Bert had ridden and bunked with a number of individuals like that. Over the years he had developed a satisfactory method of getting along with them. He made a joke now and then. He also admired Dave's old California saddle, and his beautifully silver inlaid California spurs. By the time they were within a couple of miles of the graves and were turning in behind the rearmost cattle, Bert and Dave were friends.

Snowy had demonstrated that it took him longer to forgive, or forget, but he was amiable enough as they fanned out to begin pushing the cattle westward.

The heat was coming; by midday and later it would be downright hot, but for an hour or so as the three of them hoorawhed the cattle, raising thin dust as they accomplished this, the weather was very pleasant. Once, Snowy turned back to stand in his stirrups, but if that federal lawman was still back there at the graves, the distance was too great for Snowy to make him out.

They eventually had to spread out until there was about a mile between them, because as they progressed farther westerly, the herd was dispersed. Bert was on the southernmost point and once or twice he thought he had caught a sighting of Moran and Kendall, but, again, distances were vast down here on the limitless expanse of sage country range.

There were many sassy calves. Unlike their mothers, who had been driven most of their lives and plodded along obediently as long as they were not pushed, the calves were good-feelers; without warning some of them would stick their tails in the air, throw up their heads and race away. This invariably caused the mother-cows anxiety; they would bellow and go worriedly lumbering after their babies. Usually, this caused no great problem because, even when the racing calves shot out of the herd into the open, they would suddenly dislike being alone, and would veer around and go plunging back into the herd. But it kept the wet-cows upset, and this was what the trail-drivers had to watch.

There were a number of last summer's calves, yearlings now and long yearlings, but as a rule they did not run; they were well past the age for that kind of coltishness. Usually, they had been weaned and although some still trailed their mothers, the bonds were loosening, and in many of those big yearlings there was no bond at all.

Bert made an appraisal of the cattle as he slouched along, breathing thin dust. He did not see any sore-footed critters. He did not see any weak ones either; there were a few old gummers up ahead, and their ribs would always show, but they all had the sleek shininess which came from being fat inside, fat and strong, and most of the critters, particularly the younger ones, had been piling on fat since they'd arrived on Northfield's range.

There was a lot of Longhorn in the cattle, which meant along with being long-faced and long-legged, they also had long, sweeping horns. They were the kind of cattle which would stampede blindly in a close-by lightning storm, but would not yield an inch to a predator, or a mounted man if they thought he posed a threat to a baby calf. They were fighting cattle; they had to be handled carefully, even by experienced rangemen.

Bert tried to guess the value of the herd, but it was too big and too strung out. Still he guessed it was worth a lot of money at rails'-end.

South of him a man's call came through the noise of moving cattle. Bert saw either Kendall or Moran turning up the side of the drive as he reined around to head in Bert's direction. Whoever it was broke over into an easy lope and after about fifteen minutes Bert recognised Wood Kendall, and angled slightly to effect a meeting.

Kendall's bronzed, fine-featured face held a small smile as he halted to let Bert come down to him. Where they met amid the blue sage, Kendall nodded and rested his gloved hands atop the horn as he said, 'Didn't know but what somethin' came up at the ranch and you boys might be delayed, so we left Dave to meet you, if you came along, an' me'n Wes started to work.'

Bert looped his reins to start a cigarette, and offered Kendall his makings. The older man shook his head. 'Chew,' he said, 'don't smoke.' Then he also said, 'Yesterday evenin' there was a feller prowlin' around over where you boys made them graves.'

Bert lit up and exhaled. 'Federal marshal. He had dodgers on those fellers.'

'I see,' replied Wood Kendall. 'Any reward money?'

'Yeah,' stated Bert, and added

nothing more as he changed the subject. 'With those fellers out of it there don't seem to be any reason for bunching the cattle, does there?'

Kendall looked around to where the bawling cattle were hiking through their pall of thickening dust. 'Yeah. Fact is, they been gettin' too strung out anyway. Wes and I had to ride about six, seven miles out across the sink to find a lot of 'em. That's a little more drift than we like.' Kendall turned and lifted his reins. 'I better pick up the wing a little.' He nodded and loped back the way he had come.

Bert unlooped his reins. The drag was a mile ahead. There were a few stragglers but not many, mostly cows with wobbly calves. He did not push them; there was no need, the day was still young and, as far as he knew, all the free-grazers wanted was to get their herd in a better position to be controlled without day-long riding and circling.

He was dogging it on a loose rein, drowsing in the rising warmth when he saw a brockled big cow turn back. She had a handsome set of up-curving big horns. She was a big-bodied cow, about a thousand pounds. Dave came loping southward and turned her back before she could take a little bunch with her. She was being followed by a calf as big as a long yearling but it couldn't have been nearly that old because it was still sucking. The calf was solid colour with spiky horns.

As Bert watched the big cow lower her head menacingly at Dave's approach he smiled. She was no novice at bunch-quitting. She sidestepped when Dave slacked to a walk heading for her. He turned and she sidestepped in the opposite direction. Bert had been through this dozens of times; it had always reminded him of a game of checkers; first, the cow would try something, then the rider would check her and she would try something different, and be blocked again. Depending on the pigheadedness of the cow, the game went on until the critter gave up and turned to join the herd.

That was what happened this time. Dave cut her off four times and she turned, taking her big solid-coloured calf along and went lumbering after the herd.

Dave grinned and waved. Bert waved back. He could barely see Snowy at the northernmost end of their sweep.

They covered several miles, passed the wide, grassy place where Moran and his crew had had their camp, then the cattle began slackening pace as the critters ahead were being allowed to spread out. It took a while for this to filter as far back as the drag, because the leaders were about three miles ahead, but Bert noticed the slackening off long before it got back to the drag, and eased off to allow the cattle room.

The dust thinned out, the bawling and worrying lessened, Bert turned northward, met Dave and Snowy where there were some small, two- and three-feet cut-banks, and they sat there watching as Moran came loping back down from the upper side of the drive while Wood Kendall came loping back around from the lower side.

Snowy knew this country better than the others. He was rolling a smoke when Wes Moran arrived to say it looked as though there was even better feed up ahead a few miles. Snowy inclined his head as he lighted up.

'Yeah, and it gets better all the way to the west pass through the mountains over there.'

Moran watched Snowy trickle smoke. 'Is it still Northfield grass to the west?'

Snowy flicked ash. 'Within a mile or two of those westerly mountains it is. Beyond that I got no idea who owns it, or if anyone does.'

Wood Kendall sang out sharply. The three lounging men turned. Kendall was in pursuit of that big-bodied brockled cow who was quitting the bunch and heading back the way she had come. She had her big calf alongside, and about a dozen other bunch-quitters were accompanying her. Dave swung his horse as he said, 'That old bitch,' and the three of them started eastward in a lope to make a half-circle and come down in front of the lumbering band of cattle.

It was uneven terrain, the same erosion which had at one time or another cut and carved most of the immense blue sage area made adequate footing when riding at a walk but less than adequate footing while riding at a gallop.

Bert took a less direct angle and came upon the bunch-quitters near an erosion cut-bank. He blocked the brockled cow. She did not quite halt her lumbering gallop but slackened pace to wait and see what manoeuvre the mounted man would make. He reined left and right to further confuse and discourage her.

She halted then, allowing the other bunch-quitters to crowd up as the other horsemen swung to head them off.

Bert and the brockled cow looked steadily at one another. He was certain she was not going to abandon her wish to break back. The others might, now that they appeared to have no other choice, but that big-barrelled mottled cow was not going to. He leaned to release his lariat. The alternative to losing the cow, or of abandoning her, was dangerous, strenuous—more so on the horse than the rider—and awkward, but it would work.

The others saw Bert shaking out a big loop and understood what his decision was. They, too, shook out loops and began to come in closer.

The big cow knew what the loop meant, flung herself sideways, crashing into the other cattle, and when she should have dropped her head under the other cattle, she threw it high into the air, in order to be balanced to break clear and charge. Bert made his cast from atop a little cut-bank of crumbly soil. The rope settled perfectly over those gracefully up-curving horns.

He gathered slack at the same time the cow twisted away with the full heft of her weight on the rope, which was over her back at the withers.

Bert's cincha was loose. He had been riding all morning without having occasion to step down and yank tight the latigo. Now the saddle started to turn and, instinctively, both Bert and his mount leaned as far in the opposite direction from the pull as they could, but the weight of the brockled cow pulled them, sliding sideways, toward the drop off the cut-bank, and Bert swung completely clear of the saddle on the opposite side.

The big solid-coloured calf sprang in slobbering panic to get beside his mother, and was tripped headlong by the taut rope. This additional, sudden weight pulled Bert and his struggling horse closer to the cut-bank.

Snowy was coming in from behind Bert, a big loop stretched for the cast and, southward, Wood Kendall, just starting up the cut-bank while shaking out a loop, reined to his right and also came in fast, knocking aside cattle and nearly bowling over the big cow's calf as he swept low for a heeling catch.

Kendall caught the cow by one hind leg as she was hurling all her weight into a final effort to break free, or to drag the horse and rider across the cut-bank down into the gully below.

Snowy jumped from the cut-bank's crumbling rim and made his cast as he sprang past the big cow. He, too, caught her by the horns. Dave spurred recklessly through the other lunging, stumbling cattle, made a wide cast, missed by five feet and fled past, hauling up slack to recoil the rope as Wes Moran swerved from the north and caught the cow's one free hind leg with as neat a cast as anyone had ever seen, except that at the moment he made it no one noticed.

The big cow was jerked down. She lunged to regain her feet several times and was yanked down each time. Slobber hung from her mouth, her eyes were rolling-wild. Bert yielded a little slack until his horse regained its balance, then he stepped to the ground as Snowy and Wes Moran backed clear to stretch the cow her full length, holding her helpless as Bert cast loose his rope, pushed the saddle up the ribs of his mount and turned the animal to properly reset the rig and re-cinch it. He picked up his lost hat, swung the horse to him and rose up over leather again.

The other cattle had fled in disarray,

back in the direction of the herd, taking the solid-coloured big calf with them.

Wes Moran called out. 'Dave! Cold-cock the old bitch!'

There were other ways to get those head-ropes off, but this was the quickest and least strenuous. Dave swung down, drew his Colt and went up along the back of the cow. She tried twice to get enough slack to hook him. Both times Snowy Baker backed hi horse. Dave swung his gunbarrel in a savage, chopping arc, the big cow sagged instantly, and Dave removed the head-ropes. He also removed the heel-ropes, although that was not really necessary.

He was back astride, they were all coiling their lariats, and Bert was eyeing the cow which had come very close to yanking him off the verge of the cut-bank to certain disaster, when Snowy calmly said, 'Mister Moran—about those twenty pair you owe Mister North-field...'

They all stared at Snowy, then Wood Kendall threw back his head and laughed. Wes Moran's hard features relaxed a little toward Snowy. 'Any time he wants to pick 'em out, he sure as hell is welcome to 'em.'

There was little more to be done on the blue sage prairie, once they got the old bunch-quitter on her feet and unsteadily weaving in the direction of the herd; the free-graze cattle were about where their drovers wanted them, it was turning off hot, and both Bert and Snowy were willing to head for North-field's meadow.

On the ride back Snowy said, 'Why in hell didn't you just cast off your dallies?' and Bert got red in the face before answering.

'Because I was tied hard an' fast.'

Snowy showed shock. He covered a hundred feet before speaking again. 'You always tie hard and fast?'

'No, damn it, I *never* tie hard and

fast, only this time I had a knot around the horn because the last I used that rope was to pull a tree off a trail on my way out here lookin' for work. Just didn't bother with the damned rope since then.'

When they reached the yard Bert was still angry as he and Snowy cared for their animals, then stamped over to the bunkhouse for water and a late-day meal. Snowy knew better than to bring up being tied hard-and-fast again.

After they had cleaned up, Bert's mood changed—grudgingly, but it changed. He never remained upset very long, as opposed to Snowy, who almost never got upset.

They were boiling coffee, with the bunkhouse door open to catch a breeze if one should arrive, when old Amos looked up, walked in—and smiled.

Bert had never seen Amos Northfield smile before. It did not make him look any less craggy, weathered and tough, but at least it was an improvement over his customary scowl.

They told him what they had done. They also mentioned Bert's near-disaster without going into the details of why it had happened, and when they were finished, Amos sat down at the table and began drumming on the top of it, exactly as he had done the last time the three of them had been in the bunkhouse.

Then he abruptly said, 'I said we'd talk when you boys came back. You recollect that?'

They both nodded as Amos looked from one of them to the other before speaking again.

'Well, it's taken me two days to come up with this.' He paused, looking intently at them again. 'Like I told you, the distance is too long and the weather's goin' to be too hot for Rattlesnake to ride down to California. An' I can't hardly set a saddle at all any more.'

Bert mildly said, 'What's that got to do with Rattlesnake?'

Amos's black scowl appeared instantly. 'Just shut up and listen,' he growled at Bert, and out of his shirt-front fished out something and pitched it atop the table, where the little sack fell with a very solid, almost leaden, sound.

'There's your pay for a month. I know—it hasn't been no month. I also know there's about three times as much gold in that pouch as you've earned, but I got no way of figurin' somethin' like that out—an' we don't have the time.' He paused again. 'Rattlesnake and me are goin' over to Morgansville in the morning, catch a stagecoach over there, and head for California...I can't ride and neither can he. You understand?'

Bert nodded, but Snowy just sat there favouring his sore leg, gazing fixedly at the old man, and Bert knew exactly what Snowy was thinking: Amos Northfield was crazy.

'We'll take the top-buggy,' Northfield stated, 'an' we'll leave it over there. You can pick it up some day if you've a mind to.' He dug inside his shirt again and pitched some papers atop the desk. 'Here, that piece of paper is the deed to the home-place. Those other papers are deeds to the other owned land, including all the blue sage country. And that— that's a deed to the Messican Hat cattle and brand.'

Bert and Snowy were motionless and speechless. Old Amos waited a moment, then arose to get his own cup of hot coffee, since it was obvious the pair of younger men were either unwilling or unable to move. He turned, scowling again. 'I got one other thing to give you boys...the Spanish mine.' He returned to his place at the old table. 'Now you got a payin' partnership—if you got sense enough to realise it an' work it right.' He tasted the coffee. 'The mine...You recollect me wantin' those free-grazers to move their camp?...Well, gawddammit, Snowy, don't just set there like you think I'm crazy!'

Snowy's response was given in a failing voice. 'Yeah, I recollect, Mister Northfield.'

'Well, there's a choking bunch of sagebrush growin' in a big crack in the ground in that arroyo.'

Bert nodded. 'They had to tie ropes across it to keep their horses from... That's the mine?'

The old man bobbed his head and sipped more coffee. 'I never removed the brush. It hides the shaft. Climb down through the sage. There's a couple of ladders I left there. Climb down in there; the shaft goes northward under the rocky country...Take some lanterns with you...I've taken sixty-seven pouches of pure gold out of there, an' you'll see where I quit prisin' it out of the vein. I got all I wanted. More'n I can ever use up if I live to be two hunnert.

252

Rattlesnake and I're goin' out to San Francisco and live easy for a year or so, then we're goin' up north where he's got this place in that canyon he calls Hungry Holler.'

Old Amos finished the coffee and sat there returning the stares he was getting. Eventually he arose and passed out through the open doorway before turning and saying. 'I'll tell you boys something. I got no kin. I never had no children. After my wife died I found the damned mine, and for lack of anythin' better to do I commenced sackin' up gold. What in the hell is a man in his seventies goin' to do with a lot of gold—or a lot of money for peddlin' the gold? Squeeze out maybe another six, eight years—ten at the most...Years ago, me an' my wife talked about the ranch. It was her idea. She said find a feller or a couple of partners young enough and ambitious enough to keep it goin' an' give it to 'em. That's what she said, an' Gawd bless her, that's what I'm doing...' He drew a breath and expelled it slowly. 'Rattlesnake and I'll head out early in the morning in the rig. You don't have to ride shotgun. We'll have the pouches with us.' He smiled slowly. 'Good luck, fellers.'

Snowy continued to sit like a stone for several minutes after Amos Northfield had departed, but Bert went after a cup of coffee, then tossed his hat atop the old table and sat down about where old Amos had been sitting, and put a level look upon Snowy.

'Crazy?' he asked quietly.

Snowy moved a little, considered his washed hands, considered the pouch of gold atop the table, and finally looked at Bert Osborne. 'Yeah. More'n ever, now I think he's crazy.'

Bert finished the coffee and leaned back against the table. 'I'll tell you who's crazy: You are, for not bein' able to understand that old man. Well, I'm goin' out back to the trough an take an all-over bath. You can set here an' play with that gold if you're of a mind to.'

Bert got his towel, his chunk of brown lye-soap and left the bunkhouse by the rear door, on his way round behind the barn. He paused over there in late-day shade to critically study the barn. 'One thing we got to do,' he said aloud, 'is get up there and patch that barn roof. An fix those damned corral gates so's they don't sag—and build up the carryin' capacity of Mexican Hat, an' hire a couple of men.' He strolled over to the stone watering-trough, draped his towel from a nail in the back of the log barn, and began to undress.

From the direction of the bunk-house the recognisable voice of Snowy Baker suddenly erupted in a series of wildly tumultuous shouts of exultation.

Bert went right on undressing. The only difference was that now he also started whistling.